MARR

L

REBECCA'S REVENGE

Rebecca Hind's life is thrown into turmoil when her brother mysteriously disappears and she cannot keep up rent payments for their humble cottage. Help is offered by Mr Paignton of Gorebeck Lodge, although Rebecca is reluctant to leave with him and his mysterious companion. However, faced with little choice and determined to survive, Rebecca takes the offered position at the Lodge — and enters a strange world where she finds hate and love living side by side . . .

VALERIE HOLMES

REBECCA'S REVENGE

Complete and Unabridged

LINFORD
Leicester

First published in Great Britain in 2006

First Linford Edition
published 2007

British Library CIP Data

Holmes, Valerie
   Rebecca's revenge.—Large print ed.—
Linford romance library
1. Love stories
2. Large type books
I. Title
823.9′2 [F]

ISBN 978–1–84617–795–8

Published by
F. A. Thorpe (Publishing)
Anstey, Leicestershire

Set by Words & Graphics Ltd.
Anstey, Leicestershire
Printed and bound in Great Britain by
T. J. International Ltd., Padstow, Cornwall

This book is printed on acid-free paper

1

Rebecca straightened the quilted cover on her narrow bed. Normally she would have already prepared her brother, George's, breakfast by this hour of the morning, simple a meal as it was. Then they would discuss their future and what to do about the cottage and their overdue tenancy.

Even though they had never managed to find a suitable answer to their current dilemma, they would try to think of one.

The crop had failed and they were merely producing enough to live on, but not to sell. Their last sheep had been sold.

Rebecca stared out of the cottage window up towards the moors. Where was George? He was nowhere to be found. Rebecca was becoming desperately worried about him.

Life had been very difficult since her father had left to fight Napoleon the previous spring. Together, she and George had worked hard to keep the place going so that they could pay the rent and live a frugal life, but then they received news of his death. It was a devastating blow.

George was riddled with guilt that he had been too ill to go with him. Poor Georgie, Rebecca thought, he had never been very strong. Since Father's death two months since it had been a sad and enduring time for them both.

'George, George!' Rebecca shouted, running hopefully through the cottage. Her fear grew greater each morning that he did not return. She yelled down the long corridor that joined the cottage's kitchen to their bedchambers.

Worry gnawed at her but there was no response to her call. The shutters were still closed in the kitchen and the fire unlit in the hearth. The cheese and bread left for his supper was still uneaten on the platter on the narrow oak table.

Rebecca ran to his bedchamber; she prayed she'd find him there, hopefully, just the worse for wear after a night at the Flagon Inn on the Old Moor Road. She stopped in the doorway. His bed was untouched. He had not slept in it for the third night in a row. George had not returned.

★　★　★

Her anxiety heightened when the sun rose and daylight broke the night darkness. Deep inside she felt a growing concern that George would not return. She was sure he would never run away, so where was he? What had befallen him? Rebecca put on her bonnet.

She was about to leave the cottage and walk the mile and a half to the village when she heard riders pull up outside. Two men dismounted. One she recognised as Mr Paignton of Gorebeck Lodge. She sensed something grievous had occurred but could not guess as to what could bring Mr Paignton himself to her door — unless it was to evict her personally.

She ran outside to greet them, tucking her wayward auburn curls into her bonnet as she left the sanctuary of the small cruck cottage.

'Sir.' Rebecca dipped a curtsey at Mr Paignton as he walked toward her. The other man who had dismounted with him was as dark brown as she had ever seen. She had never seen a man so coloured before. He stood quietly behind Mr Paignton. Rebecca tried not to stare.

'What brings you here, sir?' she asked nervously. 'I'm afraid my brother is not in at present. I . . . '

He raised a gloved hand, placing a finger to his lips as if to silence her.

'I am well aware of that fact Miss Hind. In fact, it is why we have come here today. Should we go inside and discuss the matter as I have some information regarding your brother's whereabouts that I must disclose to you without further ado.'

Rebecca felt her stomach tighten. She stepped back to show them into her humble home, but hesitated slightly as she saw that there was a third man outside, dressed in a great coat and black breeches. He stayed seated on his mount by the roadside.

Mr Paignton gestured towards the cottage door so reluctantly she led them in.

'Please sit down, Miss Hind . . . Rebecca,' Mr Paignton told her kindly, but in a firm voice.

'Has something happened to George, sir?' Rebecca could not bear the suspense any longer. She had to know the truth, even though she felt faint with fear at the prospect of receiving yet more bad news.

First Father's death, now had something bad happened to Georgie? Rebecca stared at the rich estate owner. His fine clothes and noble bearing seemed out of place sat on her father's old rickety chair.

'Yes, I'm afraid it has. A press gang arrived at the village two days since. They took George Hind from the Flagon Inn on their way down to Gorebeck. Samuel Diggleby and Jethro Fletcher were also pressed into service — two of our village's younger strong sons. I am trying to ascertain as to where they were taken but I fear the worst. They will not be returning until their service in HMS is completed.'

Rebecca gasped. 'But George is not strong. He will never survive! His chest ails him.' She was filled with anger because pressing men or boys into service was no less than legal abduction.

Mr Paignton shrugged his shoulders. 'These men have a job to do. Regardless of what we may think, they have the law on their side.'

Rebecca glared at him. She knew he spoke the truth that left it all the more unpalatable. There was nothing she could do though, but cope alone — somehow.

Mr Paignton spoke to her as if he was reading her thoughts. 'You must come with us, Rebecca. I shall offer you a position at Gorebeck Lodge. You will be far safer there than here. It would be impossible for you to stay here.' He stared at her pointedly. 'It is not to be considered.'

Mr Paignton placed a comforting hand on her shoulder. Rebecca was motionless, stunned by the news. Not Georgie. First Father, now Georgie! If anything had happened to Georgie she promised she would avenge his death. She would find out who was in charge of the press gang — somehow.

Someone must pay for the devastation her family had suffered. Would this war take all her family? Did it have no end in sight? As his words drifted across her she suddenly became aware of his meaning.

'No, sir. It is very kind of you to make arrangements for me, however, this is my home. It is where my brother will return to as soon as he is able. I must keep it in good order for him. I can manage it, honestly, I can!'

Rebecca looked at the well-dressed man with the slightly greying hair. A golden lion's head stood atop his mahogany cane that he slowly twirled as he spoke. He looked as if he was considering her words thoughtfully.

'Rebecca, you are entitled to stay until the end of the month. That much is paid for. I shall let you try to fend for yourself for the next two weeks. If your brother does not manage to return here to you by then, then I will keep my offer open.

'However, by the end of the month you will need to pay the tithe or forfeit the tenancy. I have Diggleby's widow and Fletcher's mother to support on the estate as it is. I can not have three tenancies unable to support themselves.' He looked at her and she thought she saw a glimmer of compassion in his eyes. 'Do you understand me, Rebecca?'

'Yes, Mr Paignton. Thank you, I shall

not let you down.'

'Good.' He patted her shoulder and nodded to his man who promptly left. 'Report to the Lodge when you've come to terms with your situation. You are too young to survive on your own and the workhouse is no place for a pretty young girl.'

'The workhouse!' Rebecca repeated the words appalled at their inference.

He nodded to her with a serious expression. 'Do not think too long about my offer, you really have little alternative.'

As Rebecca watched him leave she faced the choices open to her with a sense of challenge, but with a grieving heart for the loss of her brother, George.

2

Rebecca tried to rise to the challenge of providing for herself. Each day started before sunrise and ended after sunset. The cottage became like an empty shell to her. In her loneliness she found life incredibly hard. No more was heard about her brother. He had disappeared from her life, whisked away by government men or, Rebecca thought, legalised thieves.

Resigned to her fate she folded the rest of her meagre belongings into a trunk. Her family's possessions, few as they were, were now hidden from sight like the people themselves. A knock on the door interrupted her morbid thoughts.

She fastened the old leather strap on her small trunk and straightened her skirt to make herself presentable. Rebecca warily opened the door expecting it to be Mr Paignton's man sent to evict her.

'Rebecca, my dear child.' The high pitched voice surprised her.

'Mrs Bickerstaff, how good of you to call by.' Rebecca stood next to the door as she welcomed her surprise guest and her daughter inside the cottage. They were, she thought, the very last guests she would welcome into her home.

Mr Bickerstaff, the rector of St Ninian's church, was fortunately not accompanying his wife. She was in no mood for his dour composure or sermons on sin and retribution. Rebecca stepped back and admired their fine dresses as they entered.

They were seated uncomfortably on the old wooden chairs positioned by the empty hearth. Rebecca was wrapped in her mother's old shawl as it gave her warmth and a sense of comfort.

'Dear Rebecca,' Mrs Bickerstaff looked round the sparsely-furnished room and exaggerated a shiver. 'Emily begged me to call upon you, child.'

Rebecca looked at the pale, feminine and modestly-fashioned daughter who was two years her junior. The girl smiled nervously and Rebecca responded in kind, acknowledging the concern of a young, and by circumstances beyond their control, distant friend.

'And despite your family's disrespect of the church . . . ' Mrs Bickerstaff held up a hand, which was encased in a kid glove, to prevent Rebecca from any protest, 'I do not come to rebuke you, child, for your family's indiscretions and for their wilful neglect of the Lord and his church. We merely wish to state we hold no grudge against you — yourself.'

The earnest look on Mrs Bickerstaff's face galled and annoyed Rebecca, and yet there was a strong feeling of guilt lurking within her. Her father had turned from God when their mother had died.

Rebecca was no more than a child and remembered too little of her other than her smile and her rich red hair.

But Father had forbidden them to attend church services and so they had become the outsiders of the village, living as if on the edge of civilisation. However, they had been self sufficient. Emily and Rebecca had remained distant friends.

'My family, or should I say my father and brother, wished to offer no offence to yourself or Mr Bickerstaff. They had difficulty coming to terms with their private grief,' Rebecca answered calmly.

'It is God who they offended child! And look what has become of you as a result. Cast out, cast off and deserted by all. You can not exist like this, you are too young to become a hermit or let yourself fade away.' The older woman shook her head to stress her point, fluttering the ribbon on her secured bonnet.

'I am coping Mrs Bickerstaff,' Rebecca lied defensively, 'although I admit it is not easy.'

'Look, look!' The elder lady stood up, her eyes inspecting the room and

Rebecca's few belongings. 'Show me your hands, child.' Reluctantly Rebecca held out her hands. Recent blisters had formed as she had tried to see to all the tasks on their piece of land. She had persevered, but failed to raise enough to pay the tenancy.

'This will not do. I shall tell Mr Bickerstaff to send word to Mr Paignton this very morning. You shall take up his kindly offer immediately and leave for Gorebeck Lodge. It is no shame to be in service, particularly when you come from a disadvantaged home.'

Rebecca moved towards the door. She was not about to let this woman rule her life. She did not answer to them.

'I am grateful for your concern, Mrs Bickerstaff, but I am not ashamed of my home. There are far worse 'hovels' in the village and we have always loved and looked after our cottage well.'

'Perhaps so, but I was talking of the sin that is a stain upon it, not the nature in which it stands, more the nature of the people who have caused its and your downfall. You are still but a child. There is talk in the village that you should be admitted to either work or poorhouse.

'You have to face facts, Rebecca, you have no hope of finding a suitable suitor. It is my . . . ' she glanced at her daughter, Emily, ' . . . our wish that you be spared the shameful and unnecessary experience of being admitted to such an establishment.'

'Thank you for your concern Mrs Bickerstaff, but I am quite able to make my own decisions and . . . '

Mrs Bickerstaff raised an authoritative hand. 'Rebecca, to speak to you honestly and without any pretensions, take my advice girl and accept the position at the Lodge before the offer is withdrawn. I have spoken to Mr Paignton, who assures me he intends to give your brother the right to be a cottage tenant when or 'if' he ever returns to you.'

'He will. It's only a matter of time,' Rebecca answered, even though the words hung empty in the air, lacking conviction.

'I shall inform Mr Paignton that you will report to the Lodge tomorrow. Good day, Rebecca.' Mrs Bickerstaff walked out of the cottage before Rebecca could utter another word.

Emily hesitated, though. 'Be careful, there are those in the village who would wish to see you in the workhouse. They are jealous. It just isn't done; a young woman should not be given her own liberty. You need a husband, Rebecca.' With these parting words she followed her mother and left.

Rebecca watched them leave, walking briskly down the lane as if they were hiding where they had been. She slammed the door shut and it rebounded as if even it defied her will. Why were so many people against her?

They had always helped their neighbours when they could, but nothing they did ever changed the coldness that was shown to them when they went into the village.

★ ★ ★

Rebecca spent the rest of the day leaving her home tidy. She went to each room in turn and tried to lay her past to rest. When everything they had was in the chest and it was secured she put on her bonnet and pelisse and walked around their strip of land.

She prayed quietly and solemnly that George would return, that the bitterness that gnawed at her for his pressing would fade and that she would know inner peace once more.

For although her father had turned from their God, she had her mother's guiding faith. Hatred and bitterness were emotions that did not sit well with her, but the thought of her poor Georgie, coughing his life out upon a Man Of War, broke her heart. Before long she was heading for the woodland and the rise from where she could see

Gorebeck Lodge.

For tomorrow she had to accept an offer she did not want, in order to survive. The words of Mrs Bickerstaff had pained her. No suitor would want her, no man would consider her prospects worthy. Grimly she accepted that her future was out of her control and she had to make the best of things. It was what her family would expect of her.

After a sleepless night she walked down the long drive to Gorebeck Lodge. Approaching the large pillared doorway Rebecca nervously pulled the bell handle. Slowly it opened and a man in fine yellow livery and wig stared at her.

'Yes miss?' his voice boomed. Rebecca stood tall and managed to confidently answer his condescending tone.

'I was requested to report to Mr Paignton,' she answered honestly.

'By whom?' He looked at her in a supercilious manner questioning her words.

'By Mr Paignton himself.' She held her head high and met the man's stare.

He raised a quizzical brow. 'Do you have a card, miss?'

'Not with me,' Rebecca managed to reply calmly.

'Name?'

'Miss Rebecca Hind.'

'Wait here.' His lip curled up at one side as he re-entered the hall.

Rebecca was left to stand on the doorstep. She gazed at her surroundings, the landscaped drive, the ornamental lawns, and the impressive rearing horse fountain was breathtaking. To live in such a house Rebecca thought must be ideal.

'You are to go to the back of the house and ask the kitchen staff to take you to see Miss Jacobs. Mr Paignton is otherwise engaged. He is a busy man.'

The door was shut firmly. Rebecca looked back down the drive. She could still return to the cottage. But what was there to go back to, no family, unremitting work with little to show for it and villagers who loathed her. No, there was to be no going back.

She made her way to the servants' entrance and was shown to a small office at the back of the house. The young maid who had taken her there kept glancing at her sideways, but asked no questions. She knocked on an old wooden door.

'Enter, Millicent. Show Miss Hind in and then leave us.' The woman's voice was high-pitched with a sharp tone, and Rebecca cringed inwardly, but entered with her head held high.

'Rebecca Hind, you took your time to arrive. Well, you're here now. Where is your bag, girl?' The thin-featured woman with her grey hair pinned severely back under her starched white bonnet, stared intensely at her. 'Well, speak, girl.'

'My trunk is in the cottage. It was too heavy for me to carry. I thought it might be fetched.' Rebecca looked back at the woman who was sitting, straight-backed and looking at her disapprovingly.

20

'Did you indeed? You are definitely your father's daughter, of that I have no doubts. Your presumptions, your unruly hair and your arrogance stand in testament to it. You will be taken to a room, given a uniform, which you will look after with great care. You will then report to Cook and then you will work. Is that clear?'

'Yes. Do I receive payment for this work, ma'am?' Rebecca asked.

'You will receive the same remuneration as Millicent with whom you will share a room, less your board and you will be grateful you have been spared the ordeal of the workhouse. Your family is tainted enough. Never give me cause to complain, girl. Your alternatives are few and poor, if perhaps more befitting your station in life. Now go about your work!'

Rebecca, stunned, stared at her. She wanted to tell the woman to go to hell and back, and run from this house, the life of a servant and her past. But what could she do other than starve. She swallowed her pride and nodded; her legs would not dip a polite curtsey.

'I shall not let Mr Paignton down. Do I need to report to the butler, ma'am?' Rebecca wished she had not asked her, the moment the antagonistic question left her lips.

Miss Jacobs stood, arms folded. 'Mr Paignton's butler is in his London home attending to re-staffing in readiness for the season. You, girl, will answer to me here, or, in my absence, seek Samuel. Do not doubt my authority in this household or I shall prove to you its limits. Now go!'

3

'If ever there was a more useless excuse for a girl in this land than you, Rebecca Hind, I've yet to find one!'

Rebecca jumped to her feet nearly falling full length as she tripped on the hem of her gown. 'I'm sorry, Cook. I was dusting the books and this one fell open — I liked the print and the pretty pictures . . . '

'Put it back on the shelf before Mr Paignton knows it's been moved, and for goodness sake, pull yourself together. You've only been here a week and this is the third time I've found you dallying in his library. If Miss Jacobs catches you, you'll be out on yer ear and no messin'!'

Rebecca quickly put the book back. She dearly wanted to finish reading it because it described foreign lands, strange creatures and different peoples.

She wanted to learn as much about the world as she could. She had never known so many books existed, let alone be kept in one place.

Cook clipped Rebecca's ear, not too hard, but enough to make her flinch as she passed her on her way back to the kitchens. Although Rebecca knew she was lucky — if that were the correct phrase — not to lose her position, she hated the servitude, but anything was better than the poorhouse. She kept praying that her brother, Georgie, would soon return from the wars and she would be free to live in their cottage once more.

'I wondered where you had got to!' Miss Jacob's voice cut like a knife. It was piercing, high and filled with her own feelings of self-importance. The housekeeper stared at Rebecca.

'I was . . . ' Rebecca began but dipped a quick bob as she had learnt that Miss Jacobs demanded the utmost respect as if she owned Cartlon Grange estates rather than Mr Paignton.

'Go to the green room, remove and change the drapes, bedding and hangings. Set a fire, air it, dust it and make it ready for Mr Paignton.' Miss Jacobs glared at Rebecca as she stood, hardly able to believe the list of chores she had just received.

'By myself ma'am?' Rebecca asked in a quiet unassuming manner not wanting to have Miss Jacobs vent her anger, after receiving a clip from Cook already.

'You foolish girl! Have you no sense at all? Take Samuel with you and you'll be finished before dinner or it'll be the worst for you!'

'Yes, Miss Jacobs.' Rebecca watched the woman walk away as if she had a permanent bad smell under her nose.

'One day you'll curtsey to me,' Rebecca promised herself angrily.

★   ★   ★

Samuel was busy scrubbing pans in the kitchen. The muscular young man worked anywhere and everywhere there were jobs to be done. Rebecca had not yet spoken to him but had noticed his genial manner, no matter what the chore.

'Excuse me.' Rebecca had walked to within three feet of where he worked. He continued scrubbing and did not acknowledge her voice at all. 'Excuse me,' she repeated, 'Samuel?' She was sure he was the only one of that name working in the house.

'Miss?' He turned and quickly dried his hands.

Rebecca looked into his face noticing the warm brown eyes that looked inquiringly at her. 'Are you Samuel?'

'Yes, Miss Rebecca, didn't realise the 'excuse me' was for me.'

'Miss Jacobs told me to change the drapes and hangings in the green room. She's given me a list of tasks to do before dinner and said you were to help. If we don't finish there'll be no dinner.' Rebecca looked down, thinking there was not a chance that he would help and feeling very sorry for herself.

'Not to worry, Miss. We'll do fine.' His voice was deep, yet light of spirit and filled with optimism.

'Do you think so? I've never done this before and, to be honest, I don't know where to start. I fear you may go hungry tonight.'

'Well, miss . . . '

'Rebecca — my name, I mean.' Rebecca smiled at him warming to his manner.

'That's better, Rebecca. Now we best start work or we'll miss breakfast too.'

They went straight upstairs by the narrow servants' staircase. Rebecca noticed he seemed to have eyes everywhere. He avoided crossing the paths of the other servants. Once in the room he wasted no time in starting work. She followed his lead.

They worked tirelessly despite the dust, half-light and stifling smell of the unused room. She lit a fire in the ornately plastered hearth. It took a while but, once alight, the room warmed.

By the time they had finished she was

covered in dust and distinctly dishevelled. Her hair was a mess and her cheeks flushed from exhaustion. When the final drape was hung she was near to collapsing.

'Oh Samuel we've finished. Are we in time for dinner?' Rebecca asked hopefully.

'If we hurry I think we'll make it. You work well, Rebecca. You'll also sleep well tonight, I think.' He patted her back in a natural good-humoured way.

Rebecca responded to his friendly overture by looking up at him and grinning. He had been with Mr Paignton the morning he had visited the cottage. Suddenly he pulled his hand back as if it had been scorched.

'Thank you, Samuel. I would never have done it without you showing me what to do.'

He nodded, then quickly led the way down the stairs to the room beyond the kitchen. All the household staff were seated around the long oak table. Miss Jacobs was standing at the head. She was about to say grace. Rebecca, who had been running along the corridor, stopped dead as she arrived in the doorway of the room. She dipped slightly to Jacobs and stepped towards her place at the table.

'Rebecca Hind, what do you think you are doing?' Miss Jacobs raised her voice enough to let it crack through the air.

Once again she turned to face Miss Jacobs, resting her hands on the edge of the dresser stacked with the pewter plates and jugs, to try and help her keep control.

'We finished. All of it.' Rebecca could smell the stew from the cauldron that Cook had placed on the rest at the end of the table. Each person had a piece of bread ready on his or her plate. Rebecca was so hungry she stared at hers. Miss Jacobs came over to Rebecca's plate, picked it up and offered it to another maid.

'Muriel, put this back in the store. Rebecca will not be eating with us tonight.' Jacobs gazed at Rebecca's disbelieving expression.

'But why? I've finished. We did everything you asked us to.'

'You insolent girl! How dare you come to the dinner table in such a state! Look at you, your hair's a mess. You are a disgrace. You would eat the good Lord's food without washing first?' She paused momentarily as she exchanged a look of disgust with Samuel.

'But Miss Jacobs, we only just finished in time and . . . '

'For your insolence and disregard of our wishes you shall forego your dinner. Clean yourself up, change uniform, then launder your dress. You will clear the table and wash the pots before you return. Ask the Lord's forgiveness and perhaps tomorrow you will show more respect. This is a God fearing household, not a country midden.'

Rebecca took a step away. She looked around at the faces of some of the other staff. Some smirked, some looked down avoiding eye contact, but no-one spoke out. Miss Jacobs' word was law.

She ruled the servants with an iron rod.

Anyone who had the nerve to cross her answered to Mr Paignton. No-one wanted that. Rebecca humiliated, tired, frustrated and angry left and ran across the cobbled yard to her room beyond the dairy. She only possessed one other dress.

Opening the wooden door she climbed the stairs that led to the room that she shared with Millicent, a girl of simple wit. Pretty, but slow. Rebecca prayed that her brother would return soon, that they would beat Napoleon and life could return to normal. If only Father had not been killed in the wars.

She no longer had time to walk in the fields, paddle by the stream or sit and watch the rabbits play as she had before. Now life was one long discipline.

Tears of frustration welled up within her as she changed even though she realised she had more to be thankful for than many. It was the thought of her Georgie being dragged away that filled her with anger every time. Did she hate her own country? Her thoughts were so confused because she just wanted him back.

She looked longingly at her bed and sighed. Somehow she would adapt, she would survive. They would not beat her. Rebecca made her way to the laundry room. Two hours later she had washed her dress and hung it on the huge frames that were raised above the grooved stone floor. She had then faced the pile of plates left for her to wash in the kitchen.

Finished and famished she walked out into the night air. The rest of the servants had retired. She sat on the small wall that marked out the herb garden and stared at the stars. The sky was clear of cloud and the air still. One star shone brighter than the rest. She wondered why.

'Here.' The deep voice surprised Rebecca and she jumped to her feet.

Her head felt dizzy and she nearly lost her balance. Two strong arms encircled her.

'It's only Samuel. Come with me.' He led her behind the kitchen buildings to one of the storehouses. Rebecca hesitated. 'It's all right, Miss Rebecca.' He let go of her arm. 'Trust me.' She found herself wondering about his age, probably some years older than her twenty.

'Where do you want me to go and why?' she whispered.

'Just in here. I heard you was hungry and I have a pie, some milk and a cake. You interested or are you going to let that bully run you into the ground? She will if you don't outwit her.'

Rebecca went inside the storehouse. Samuel unshuttered a lamp and showed her a platter. 'You eat it quick, miss, and then get as much sleep as you can. No more gazing at the stars. She is out to break your spirit.'

'Why? I've never done anything to her other than to do what she ordered.

I've only been here a week. What can she have against me?' Rebecca ate the food.

Her stomach felt quite ill with the first few bites she swallowed, she was so hungry.

'You're young and pretty. Your eyes have spirit. She don't much like that.' He sat cross-legged on the floor in front of her.

She was perched on the top of a small keg. Rebecca had never been alone with a strange man before, black or white, in such a fashion. If she was discovered she would be labelled for life. She shuddered at the thought.

'You take care, Rebecca. Finish off and go straight to your room. I'll watch your back as much as I can, but you have to act subdued. Don't answer back and keep your eyes looking down if you feel anger.'

'Samuel, why would you watch my back?' Rebecca asked and watched his face break into a smile again.

'Well let's say I don't like people

being broken down and I owe an old friend. Besides . . . ' he said jovially, 'not many folk 'excuse' themselves for me. You go now and take care.' He was watching her as if he knew her. His whole manner was familiar, in the way of an old family friend, yet still she knew she had never met him before.

'Thank you, Samuel.'

Rebecca gulped down the milk, rubbed her lips and, leaving quickly, she ran all the way back to her small room.

'Where's you been?' Millie asked.

'Staring at the stars,' Rebecca answered honestly.

'Whatever for?' Millie look tired and bemused.

'They're beautiful,' Rebecca answered.

'Well you wish you hadn't tomorrow. Miss Jacobs says you to get up and set the table for breakfast so you best sleep now.'

Rebecca felt her heart sink at the thought of so little sleep, but at least she had a full stomach and a friend. No matter what Miss Jacobs did, she would not be broken! If she had to serve then she would until she was rescued by her brother, or . . . well, she decided she would think about the 'or' later.

4

The following weeks followed a similar pattern. Long days, always filled with rebukes by Miss Jacobs. If it were not for Samuel, she would have had to exist on the most meagre of meals.

Somehow, somewhere, he always managed to help her. He would appear in corridors or rooms and aid or feed her. It was as if he was a guardian angel, but she felt like she did not deserve one. As time passed and George did not return, her desire for vengeance against his abductors grew.

Eventually, Miss Jacobs seemed to tire of the daily vigil over her and she was left to a more normal routine. Rebecca always appeared subdued in Jacobs' presence. Looking down to hide her true feelings. She felt this had helped to appease her ego.

'Rebecca, you are to go to Miss

Jacobs in the rose garden,' Millicent said urgently to Rebecca as she laid the table.

'Rose garden? Why there? Am I to tend gardens now too?'

'How am I to know? All I do is pass on orders. You best hurry. It took me a while to find you,' Millie said as she took over Rebecca's chores.

Rebecca left the house and walked quickly through the archway from the fountain garden to the rose garden. Mr Paignton was sitting on a stone seat. She adjusted her cotton bonnet.

'Ah, Rebecca, come sit with me a moment.' He patted the seat next to him.

'Sir?' She stepped forward somewhat hesitantly. 'I was told to see Miss Jacobs.'

'Well, you are seeing myself.'

'Has something happened?' Rebecca could not understand why after a few months in the house with no contact with Mr Paignton himself he should summon her in such an irregular manner. She thought he had forgotten about her presence at the lodge.

'Don't be frightened, Rebecca.' He looked into her pale green eyes and held his hand out for hers. She gave it with some apprehension. 'You are the image of your dear mother, Esther. She was the prettiest girl in the village at your age. I remember her like it was yesterday. Your hair is not quite as rich in its auburn hues but it curls in just the same way. When she married your father he was the envy of every red-blooded man around.'

Rebecca flushed deeply. She had never had a man describe her in such a forward fashion and rarely had anyone mentioned her mama.

'I embarrass you, child. I meant only to flatter.' He pulled her to the seat and patted it so that she felt she should sit down next to him.

'No, sir. It is just that I had no notion that you even knew my mother,' Rebecca said, not wanting to admit how embarrassed she felt for, other than her father, no-one had ever complimented her mama.

'My family did not always have wealth, Rebecca. We were never poor, but my father worked hard to build up a woollen trade and I was fortunate to benefit by always having a comfortable home, unlike your own.' He stared at her with such a strange, yet apparently knowledgeable understanding of her family.

'My home was comfortable enough. It was filled with love. We had food on the table and Mother and Father and my brother were happy until . . . ' She gazed at the peach rose next to the seat.

'Until she died.' He patted her knee and she did not know where to look as his hand lingered a moment longer than seemed appropriate.

'Poor Rebecca. And then your father . . . ' he sighed, ' . . . but he died a hero fighting Boney and you should be proud of him.'

'I am.' Rebecca nodded immediately.

'Yes, well of course you would be.

Rebecca you are so young to have had so much tragedy in your life, but there is more I must tell you. Your brother is missing, presumed to be dead.'

Rebecca gasped and put her hand to her mouth as the horror of his words sank in. It could not be. She told herself over and over again. 'It must be a mistake.' She spoke the thought out loud.

Mr Paignton had both her hands in his. 'Dear Rebecca, I should not have had to tell you this awful news, but I feel it is my duty, as your father worked on this estate for many years.

'Of course,' he shook his head as if readying himself to speak the inevitable, 'this means that your cottage will never be your home again and so I'm offering to make your position here more permanent.'

'But you said he was missing. He may still be alive, sir. No-one knows for sure.' She held both his hands as she rose to her feet with conviction. 'We must believe he is alive if there is the smallest chance that he could be.'

His grey eyes stared into hers and for one moment she saw a strange glint in them. Was it hope, or something else? She did not know, but Rebecca was suddenly aware of their position. Master and servant, standing holding hands and staring into each other's eyes in the most intimate fashion. She released her grip and took a step backwards. 'I'm sorry, sir, I forgot myself.'

'No, Rebecca, you are quite correct.' He stood up. Although his hair was greying and he was almost the same age as her father he still had a youthful stance and a good physique. He always dressed smartly and it accentuated his tall straight stature. 'It is I who am insensitive. I will presume he will return one day; however, the cottage and the tenancy have been let. Are you content here Rebecca?'

Rebecca hesitated before answering. 'I am indeed grateful that you have given me a position, sir.'

He patted her shoulder. 'Good, because the workhouse is no place for such a pretty girl as yourself. Now, you can spend a few moments in the chapel to compose yourself before returning to your duties.' He smiled at her, but she was aware that his eyes were roaming farther than her face.

'Thank you, sir.' Rebecca backed away, before turning and running to the chapel. Her mind was in turmoil. Was her brother really dead? Was she the only existing member of her family? No, she wouldn't believe it was so. She could sense Mr Paignton was still watching her and she couldn't wait to enter the peace of the chapel.

Once inside the chapel she paused, uneasy at the way he had looked at her. The words he had spoken were kind and had been filled with admiration for her mother. She did not know why. When he'd commented on her own looks it had unnerved her.

She tiptoed across the wooden floor and it creaked gently under her feet.

This was part of the old house, built in Tudor times and it was sparse, except for its stained glass windows at the gable end. An open Bible lay on the covered altar and she looked down at the text, *There is a time for everything.* Ecclesiastes informed her.

When would her time come to be happy again and once again feel loved? When would the injustice of Georgie's situation be punished? The pews were old. The servants were often summoned for standing services and sermons delivered by Reverend Jonah Donnelly, an old gentle man who Rebecca thought had a kindly face and countenance.

She sat down in the pew before the altar and remembered her family, feeling a heavy isolation and unease. Where was her hope, her future now? 'Dear Lord, give me back my brother, please.'

'Miss Jacobs is looking for you. She heard you've been talking to Mr Paignton in the gardens.' Samuel's voice did not make her jump like it had at first because she frequently did not hear him come near, but was pleased to see his friendly face.

'My brother might be dead, Samuel. Mr Paignton told me. The cottage will no longer be our home even if he returns.' She gazed at the altar.

'Well, Miss Rebecca, if he might be dead, he might also be alive.' He put a comforting hand on her shoulder.

'That's what I said, Samuel. I'll never give up hope unless I know for sure.'

'Now that is what is known as faith.' He sat down next to her in the pew and Rebecca thought how he always appeared to be calm and relaxed as if he had a sense of peace within him.

'How long have you worked here, Samuel?'

'Eternity, or so it seems at times. I can barely remember a time when I wasn't here and, if I told the truth, I prefer it that way.'

For a moment his smile was gone and he looked serious and much older.

Rebecca found it difficult to guess his age, possibly he was the same age as Mr Paignton.

'How did you come to be working for Mr Paignton?' Rebecca asked and was surprised when Samuel immediately stood up.

'Miss Rebecca, we have work to do — can't stay chatting here all day. What would Miss Jacobs say, eh?'

5

Rebecca washed, cleaned, scrubbed and polished for the next month. Her days started early and invariably finished late. There was little free time and she never had the chance to venture into the library.

It was as if Miss Jacobs had decided to keep her enclosed within the kitchen and servants' halls. Until one day, Miss Jacobs had taken to her bed, an unheard of event. She had a bad chill and had been told to rest. Millie and Mrs Howell, the cook, were at her beck and call, but Rebecca found she had lighter duties, shorter hours and even the majority of a morning to herself.

Quietly she left the kitchen, crossed the cobbled yard, passed by the end of the stable block and slipped into the cover of the woods. She looked at the new shoots, the bluebells and breathed deeply and imagined that the new life was filling her tired body, rejuvenating her so that she became once more Rebecca Hind, young and free instead of the caged bird she had felt like.

Following the narrow path through the elm, oak and hazel she found old stepping stones leading across a rippling stream. Rebecca crossed and ambled along the bank side path as it twisted and turned down stream. Even when it became no more than slippery stone steps at the side of a small waterfall she carefully manoeuvred her way.

The sight of the pool that surrounded the fall made her want to dangle her hot feet in the clear water. It was a sheltered spot and she couldn't see why she shouldn't.

She made her way to a place under a willow. Just as she was about to step into the stream there was a large splash and she jumped back.

She watched for the cause of the break in her tranquillity and saw before her a sign not befitting a young lady, for a man had jumped into the pool from a rock. Rebecca stood with her back to the trunk of the tree. Its branches hung before her like a curtain between her and the sunlit pool.

If she ran she would be seen. If she stayed she would see far more than she ought to, yet her fascination and curiosity prevented her from covering her eyes or moving.

She watched in admiration as he pulled himself back up on to the rock. His muscular body reminded her of the garden statues that adorned Mr Paignton's gardens. He stood, tall and proud, unaware he was the object of her scrutiny, then dived in again.

He disappeared into the depth of the water before surfacing and swimming across to the bank near her tree.

She held her breath. Panic filled her yet it was mingled with a strange feeling of excitement. He rested his arms on the bank not two yards in front of her, his eyes watching the waterfall. His dark wet hair clung to his head as he ran his fingers through its length. She looked upon him and realised he was the man she had last seen outside her own home the day after George had been taken.

'Luke, if you're through playing, perhaps we can talk business.'

Rebecca slowly breathed out as the man swam to the other bank. Mr Paignton was standing, fully dressed, on the rock. He watched the man's form climb out of the river without saying a word or offering a hand to help him. Not that he needed any. Rebecca could not move.

She watched and admired both the stance and dress of Mr Paignton who carried himself well for a man of some maturity and guiltily she could not help but admire the physique of the younger man, who dressed as the two talked. She could not hear a word that was spoken, only the muffled sound of their voices.

An hour must have passed by as the men reclined on the rock beneath the sun and talked. She waited until finally they stood up once more. The man in black shook Mr Paignton's hand and the master of the house left. The stranger followed some moments later and Rebecca decided to risk the climb back up the path. It took her much longer than her descent and she was quite out of breath when she finally reached the level ground at the top of the fall.

The view from this point was breathtaking as she looked down the river's meandering path through the wooded valley below. How she wished she could have stayed and watched until the light faded and the stars came out, but no, she must return to the kitchens.

She thought of the vision by the pool. Who was he? She would ask Samuel.

She stepped on to the path that would lead her through the woodland and back to the house. She had not taken but two paces though, when a dark figure stepped out in front of her.

His fashionable hat, the black coat and trousers, the moisture on his hair all told her that this was unmistakably the man she had observed. He smiled, she stared, but neither spoke for a moment.

'Good day, sir.' She boldly looked straight at his face. Her flushed cheeks betrayed her true sense of unease. She prayed he had not seen her by the pool.

'Tell me, miss, are you a rabbit that hides in a hole?' He casually rested his hands upon a black walking stick. It was, like himself, quite impressive being made of a long twisted piece of blackthorn.

'I beg your pardon, sir? I am no rabbit. I merely walk in the woods for exercise and pleasure.' She forced her eyes to meet with his. They were full of character, if not openly teasing her there was certainly some merriment there. Yet despite the man's build and manner she sensed there was no malice.

'And has this walk been pleasurable, miss?' He put his head on one side and raised a brow enquiringly.

'You must excuse me. I must return to my duties before I am missed.' Rebecca side-stepped so as to pass him.

'No, miss,' he turned without trying to prevent her passing, 'you excuse me. For I take great pleasure in both nature and in the woods. May I suggest that in future you amble up stream, unless you find the views beneath the fall particularly appealing to the eye.' He had been speaking earnestly, but then a smile crossed his face as if he could not prevent it.

'I can assure you, sir, I . . . I . . . ' Rebecca was lost for words and as the man burst into spontaneous laughter she quickened her step and continued upstream running as she neared the house. Although she was far too embarrassed to have answered, she found herself grinning shamelessly.

Samuel greeted her. 'Where have you been, Rebecca? Cook has shouted for you for nearly two hours. Go freshen yerself and get a clean apron before you see her.'

She stepped inside, but Samuel took her arm. 'Best take off your boots an' I will clean 'em for you while you change.'

Rebecca looked at the state of her only pair of boots. They were caked in mud. 'Thank you, Samuel,' she said gratefully and ran to her room. By the time she'd brushed her hair, dressed ready to return to the kitchens, Samuel met her in the yard with a pair of polished boots.

'You're in a lot of bother again.' He handed her the boots, but before he released them he added, 'Be careful where you walk.'

'Samuel, who was the man who came with Mr Paignton to my cottage?' Rebecca pulled her boots on quickly not looking directly at Samuel's face as she did not want to incur more interest in her casual enquiry.

'He's of no importance to you. I suggest you see Cook before Miss Jacobs hears her screams.'

6

Miss Jacobs did not fully recover from her ailment and Rebecca was increasingly called upon to help with her duties. She was the only house servant who had been taught her numbers, could read and write. Rebecca was so relieved to be released from some of her interminable duties in the kitchens and Cook's unreliable temper that she became a most studious assistant.

'Rebecca,' Miss Jacobs appeared in the doorway of the room she shared with Millicent. This was a rare sight as Miss Jacobs now walked with a stick and never entered servants' rooms.

Rebecca must have shown her surprise on her face. Miss Jacobs smiled, which was, Rebecca thought, an even more unusual and too rare a sight. 'I have not died, girl. This is me in the flesh not some shocking apparition of one of those dreadful new novellas.'

'Sorry, Miss Jacobs, it is just you rarely . . . '

'Rebecca, I have never come here, as well you know.' Miss Jacobs pointedly stared at the mess on Millicent's side of the room, then more approvingly at the neat bed, hung uniform and orderly side table that was Rebecca's side of the sparsely decorated room. 'Which, for Millicent, is just as well it appears although I shall be having words with her. However, that is not the reason I have inconvenienced myself to be here. I want to speak to you about your situation here.'

Rebecca brought the only chair for Miss Jacobs to sit on. She sat gratefully and graciously rested her hands on her stick.

'You have worked well, despite my initial misgivings about you and your . . . heritage.'

'My heritage?' Rebecca queried.

'Yes, your unfortunate parentage of which I shall say no more. Please do not interrupt again.' Miss Jacobs fixed one of her reproachful stares upon her that she would have cringed under the influence of six months ago. 'You have worked hard and been most respective of my instruction. That is why I have recommended to Mr Paignton that you . . . ' she swallowed, 'replace me.'

Rebecca thought she actually saw a tear escape from the corner of Miss Jacobs' eye, but if she did it was quickly brushed away with one index finger.

'Replace you?' Rebecca did not believe what she was hearing.

'Yes. I will be leaving this place and staying with my sister. Mr Paignton will be virtually closing the house for the winter and will need a skeleton staff here. His brother may be staying part of the time. He comes and goes at will, but his demands are few. He must not be pestered, girl. He keeps his own company and doesn't want a chit of a girl chasing around.

'Mind, there's enough in the village who would, particularly that Bickerstaff girl. But that's none of our affair. Don't think I have done you any favours, Rebecca. This house, Gorebeck Lodge, is vibrant when in season but desolate when closed.

'This is a lonely place. It suits Mr Luke admirably for he has a sombre demeanour, unlike Mr Paignton. You are but twenty. You should be finding a husband and having children of your own, not keeping house for the ghosts of long past.

'However, we can not dictate our own destiny, that is in the hands of the good Lord and he has been most generous to you despite your parentage. Still our Lord works first among sinners.'

Rebecca looked aghast at Miss Jacobs' openness. She could not believe the change in her manner towards her.

'You have little prospect of finding yourself with anyone but a farmhand and somehow I think you would prefer the company of Mr Paignton's books. He will speak to you in the morning then he shall inform the rest of the staff as to who will stay and who will go.

'I have already been informed that I am not fit or able enough to do the duties that I have filled in the past twenty-five years! Still, what will be will be and I do miss my sister and the sea.'

'Miss Jacobs will you return when the master does?' Rebecca asked, not believing that the elder woman could be so easily dismissed after serving so long.

'No, that I will not. This house has had too much of my life already. Take care it does not take too much of yours.'

'I am nearly one-and-twenty. I have a lot of time ahead of me.'

Miss Jacobs merely looked at Rebecca's cheerful response.

'Pack your belongings. You shall be moved into the house. You may now sleep in the room adjacent to mine. Two dresses have been hung ready for you and some decent boots.

'From tomorrow, you will answer

59

only to Mr Paignton, myself and will be equal to Cook. Move your things and report to Mr Paignton by eight o'clock in the morning. Take the rest of the day to think about what I have said.' She stood to go.

'Thank you, Miss Jacobs,' Rebecca said genuinely.

'Don't. I can see you are different to your mother. She was flighty. I was too quick to judge you.' She left.

★ ★ ★

Rebecca did as she was instructed. Her new room had a carpet, matching bedcover and curtains, drawers, a looking glass and chest. A washstand with matching chair and table were next to the window that overlooked the woodland; she felt suddenly drawn towards it.

She put her meagre belongings away neatly and ran down the back stairs wearing her old boots, and into the woods. She had not seen much sunshine for a long time except in brief glimpses through the windows and, as she crossed the yard, the warmth filled her with a sense of freedom.

'Oh God, let my brother, Georgie, return soon. Thank you, Lord, for setting me free!'

To Rebecca that was what it felt like. She had been given time and space. She would be able to roam the estate, almost at will. All would be well, her brother would return and she would be here waiting for him.

Her head was so filled with Miss Jacobs' news, she had automatically followed the path that led to her friendly willow. She suddenly remembered the stranger in black.

She looked around, but today there was no sign of him. She looked longingly at the pool and, just as she had intended on her previous visit, she removed her boots and dangled her legs in the cool water. It felt like heaven on earth. How she wished she dared to do as the stranger had done.

'So you decided to venture here once again.'

The voice was unmistakable; she had heard no-one coming, yet he was here. 'Sir, I thought I was alone.' She lifted her feet on to the bank beneath her skirts and picked up her boots.

'Please, I did not wish to disturb you. I merely did not wish you to think I would simply stand by and stare.' He looked straight into her eyes, but she was too ashamed to keep his gaze.

'Perhaps, sir, you did not fear my reaction to discovering your presence? I could hardly assault or overpower you.'

She forced herself to meet his eyes. She was relieved to see he did not mock her, but nodded in agreement.

'You could be right and I do not suppose for one minute that, if you purposely wished to flaunt yourself, you would come to such a secluded spot. No-one would, would they, Miss Rebecca?'

'No, sir.' Rebecca could not help herself feeling comfortable in the stranger's presence, but she realised he had used her name. 'How do you know my name? We have not been introduced.'

'That is true, Rebecca Hind. However, I make it my business to know these things.'

'Then you have the advantage of me. Who are you?'

'You must excuse me, I have engagements to keep and I fear I am late. Good day, miss.' He nodded politely and moved away quickly.

Rebecca instinctively went to follow him, to continue their conversation and receive an appropriate answer to her query, but she quickly realised that her feet were still unshod. By the time she had pulled on her boots he had disappeared from sight.

Frustrated, she made her way towards the house, her peaceful feeling lost by the stranger's knowledge.

She stopped outside the Lodge and looked at the façade. Her life had taken another turn. She was to be housekeeper of this grand home. She couldn't help but compare this time with her arrival after the Bickerstaffs' visit to her cottage.

The trepidation she had felt then was very different to the small bubble of excitement she could feel now. What else lay in front of her only God knew, but Rebecca believed that she had found the strength and resolve to get her through almost anything.

7

Rebecca arose early one morning. She felt as though she was in hiding at the Lodge. The fact that she had left the cottage and the village so quickly had left her with a feeling of sadness and regret; as though she were hiding in shame from the Bickerstaffs and the other villagers. So Rebecca decided to put her demon to bed and face them.

She walked boldly down the lane towards the village seeing no reason why she shouldn't hold her head high and show off her new clothes, the status of her position of which she had become quite proud.

The village was small and the people who lived within it existed on what gossip was brought in by traders — the fishermen from the coast, wool merchants from the country, monks with their home-made tonics or passing peddlers. People didn't venture far themselves.

However, Rebecca wanted to be different; she desired to see the world. The books in the library that she had read were full of descriptions of strange new lands. Or even the old ones, like France. She sighed heavily as that was one land she never wanted to visit.

Memories of the day her father had left the cottage flooded her mind. No, she would not go there. Rebecca shook her head defiantly as if erasing all the sad thoughts or doubts that had haunted her.

It was time, she reasoned to lay her ghosts to rest. She had nothing to be ashamed of, but as she approached her old cottage, the only home she had ever really known, her heart felt heavy and was beating hard in her chest.

Then she realised that the door was slightly open and she thought she saw movement within the cottage. She stared at the window. Yes, there it was again. She ran the rest of the way, bursting through the door with such energy and joy, shouting, 'Georgie! Georgie — when did you get back, I . . .'

Rebecca, stopped dead in her tracks. Disbelief hit her hard as she stared at Emily Bickerstaff laying the table before a newly-fitted range. The fine linen on the table and matching crockery, like the chairs and furnishings were all new.

'Rebecca, I was not expecting you. I was going to write and invite you once we were settled.' Emily looked nervously around her at all her new possessions.

'All along you wanted my home. Would you have gone to any lengths to have it? The stories about the workhouse, the village's jealousy were lies. It was you all along. You would have seen my ruin in order to move in here.' Rebecca saw the bedroom door was slightly ajar.

'No, no, you mustn't think like that! They were true, what the people were thinking . . .'

'Who gave them the idea? You?'

'No, no it wasn't like that, honestly. I wanted to help, I did . . . but Jeremiah and I were to marry and Mama thought that as this cottage was near to the rectory and was the largest in the village it would be perfect for us until the new terrace in the village is completed. There would not have been room for you as well . . . it would have been awkward.

'Then of course we should move to a proper home as soon as our real home was complete. This is just a stop gap.' Emily coloured. She nervously put the last spoon down and wiped her hands on a cloth.

Emily looked extremely flushed, but all Rebecca could feel was sheer anger and disgust that her friend would seek so low as to plot to have her turned out of the only home she had ever known — and at such a sad time for her.

'This was a proper home — it was my home!' Rebecca almost shouted at her in a barely controlled voice filled with fury.

'Well not anymore, my girl!' Mrs Bickerstaff's voice echoed around the room and Emily visibly shook as her mother entered from the bedchamber. 'How dare you burst in to my daughter's house unannounced and accuse my poor Emily of such a thing, and in her condition too.'

She moved around her daughter, placing an arm on the young woman's shoulders protectively, looking far too smug for Rebecca's liking.

'What do you mean 'her condition'?' Rebecca looked at Emily scrutinising her stature and poise. 'You are to have a child . . . already?' Rebecca asked incredulously without thinking of the inference of her words.

Mrs Bickerstaff's face turned a deep shade of puce. 'How dare you infer such a slur on my poor Emily. She is a lady, unlike you, miss. Emily is from a respectable family; not the daughter of a wanton woman, a harlot, like you are yourself.'

Rebecca considered Mrs Bickerstaff's

attack was wicked. Her eyes were filled with hatred and her vitriolic words cut through Rebecca's heart like a knife. She tried to maintain her composure, but it was a struggle under such a severe attack.

Rebecca paused. She had been brought up short by the woman's evil words, but she would not lower herself to her level by responding in kind. 'I did not infer anything, nor did I mean any disrespect to her. It is just that such a lot has happened in such a short period of time. I apologise, Emily, if my words offended you, they were not intended to.'

Emily nodded as if to accept Rebecca's apology. But the expression of guilt on the girl's face was as good as a confession. Emily had nearly brought the good name of Bickerstaff into disrepute. It must have been a swiftly arranged wedding.

'Now if you, Mrs Bickerstaff, will apologise for your repeated slurs on my dead mother's character then I shall leave and no more will be said on either matter.' She stared defiantly back at Mrs Bickerstaff copying the attitude she had witnessed Miss Jacobs use so many times on her.

'I will not say any such thing. Your mother's reputation goes before her, even beyond the grave, Rebecca Hind. Surely you must be aware of the truth by now?' Mrs Bickerstaff's composure and confidence was starting to undermine Rebecca's but she maintained her stern look.

'You should not speak ill of the dead for they cannot defend themselves. As wife to the vicar I would have expected better of you.'

Rebecca's words struck at Mrs Bickerstaff's heart; the girl stood her ground as the older woman crossed the room to her. She would never be disloyal to the memory of her beloved mama — what small memory she had of her she would protect to her last breath.

'Listen, you foolish girl. Your mother

was the mistress of Mr Paignton and everybody in the village knew it. She thought herself better than the rest of us and used her body to gain this cottage. Only men with no faith like your father would even dare to live with such a woman. He had no pride nor moral fibre. They were in many ways a perfect couple, completely deserving of each other. And have you stepped into the 'position' now?'

Rebecca stared back at her in disbelief. The woman was beyond contempt. Was there no low she would stoop to, to discredit her family.

'You lie. How dare you. Your mind is filled with filth,' Rebecca replied adamantly. 'I do not know what has possessed you, but it sounds like the words of the devil himself have entered your head. You should be ashamed of yourself.'

'No, girl, I do not lie. Unless you repent you and your brother are destined to join your parents in Hell.'

Rebecca took in a deep breath. 'Then

we shall indeed meet again, Mrs Bickerstaff.' The woman took in a gasp of air. Rebecca turned to a tearful Emily. 'Goodbye!'

Mrs Bickerstaff's tirade was explosive as Rebecca left the familiar cottage for what she knew would be the last time. Each step she took was quicker than the last until she was running.

Tears threatened to stream down her face, but she held them back. She would not be undermined by such a woman. How could she lie so? To what purpose?

She had already taken the cottage from her so there was no reason to say such wicked things about her mother? What had her parents done to Mrs Bickerstaff that deserved such a vicious attack on their characters and her memories?

★   ★   ★

Two hours later Samuel found her in the chapel still wearing her bonnet and pelisse.

'Miss Rebecca, whatever are you doin' breakin' your heart in here?' He looked at her with a compassionate and friendly expression that nearly caused her resolve not to break down to falter.

She had no tears to shed, her eyes were red, her throat sore. Rebecca had not cried for over an hour and she doubted she ever would again. Her resolve to rely only on herself and never be hurt by anyone's words again was all but complete. She shook her head not wanting to repeat Mrs Bickerstaff's vile words to him.

'Miss, you know sometimes even the worst things aren't so bad when you share them with a friend. Share your pain with me and let Samuel help sort it out. What can be so bad that it has touched you so?' He looked into her eyes with his deep brown ones and despite her decision not to she told him, even though it hurt her deeply to repeat the words.

'Oh, Miss Rebecca.' He shook his head and looked away a moment.

'I know her words were lies but . . . '
Rebecca stared at him. His facial
expression, the shift of his stance,
uneasy and nervous could only mean
one thing. 'You know something about
this, don't you?'

Rebecca asked hardly able to believe
the look on his face. It was not one of
surprise. He obviously knew something
and Rebecca felt her heart sink at the
faint fear that there was even an iota of
truth in it.

'I won't lie to you, Rebecca. But
sometimes the truth isn't what we want
it to be. Now, in my own life my
greatest sorrow was being ripped from
my mama's arms as a wee child. I can
still hear her screams in my dreams.
The cries don't seem like they'll ever
fade. I don't dream them every night,
but sometimes I do, even at my age.

'Now listen, your mama was a good
woman. She was kind, loving and like
you, very beautiful. She loved your
father more than her own life, more
than her own soul. He was injured

badly in a farm accident. She had no money for decent medicine. It was a hard time for everyone then as now.

'Mr Paignton paid for it, he saw that your father had all the care he needed, but it took the best part of a year before he was fit to work the land again. Your mother and Mr Paignton saw each other frequently throughout that time.

'He was besotted with her. Neither of them meant anything to happen. Well, your mama certainly didn't even though he turned her head with gifts and things. She was very flattered.

'Both were married, happily, but sometimes things just happen. Your mother was a passionate woman, not a harlot. She needed a man. I don't know who told on them, but word reached the village. Your papa took it very badly and he didn't learn to forgive your mama until it was too late. Then she became ill herself with a fever that no amount of money could cure and she died.

'He, your papa, was a bitter man

after that, and Mr Paignton was a broken man — he was never quite the same again.'

Samuel looked at the altar for a few moments and Rebecca did not think it was fitting for her to comment. He was deep in his own thoughts. She waited until he spoke once more. 'He took you in because he felt he owed your mama. That's the honest truth of it . . . I'm sure.'

Rebecca stared at him, his words echoing inside her head. Mrs Bickerstaff had not known the facts, her mind had painted in the deepest shadows into the unknown. Rebecca could not change the facts of it that alone stood for themselves. Her mother had been a kept woman — a wife and a rich man's mistress.

'No,' Samuel continued, 'he did it, for he loved her dearly, but could not show you favour until now or it would set more gossip going, so you were set to work without favour.'

Rebecca swallowed. 'So that is why

you have been looking after me when I weakened, and why Miss Jacobs seemed to hate me on sight. You cared for me because you were ordered to.'

'Yes and no, Rebecca. Miss Jacobs was ordered to be firm but fair.' He smiled at her and she responded in kind. She felt as though she had been the unwitting pawn in some kind of charade.

'Will you be leaving with Mr Paignton or staying here when he goes?' Rebecca was fond of Samuel. He had been a true friend to her. The thought of him leaving her, too, filled her with great sadness.

'Yes miss, I go where Mr Paignton goes. That is my purpose in this life.' Samuel patted her on the back. 'You'll be fine, Rebecca. The villagers have no place here nor you there. Stay separate until we return next year. You can attend chapel, and winter will soon pass. You've all them books to read your way through. Yer ma was just the same that way. She loved to learn and always

asked the mister lots of questions.'
Samuel looked again at the altar.

'You were fond of her, too, weren't
you?' Rebecca asked.

'Yes, she was special, like you. A lady
who was born into the wrong place
maybe. Perhaps even the wrong culture,
but then that's a whole different
argument. But you'll do better.' He
stood up.

'You go and wash your face and
make yourself nice and smart again. You
have to see Mr Paignton before he
goes.'

'No, I can't. Not now. How can I face
him knowing what has gone before? It
wouldn't be proper.' Rebecca gazed at
her hands as if bewildered by the
thought.

'You'll do no such thing. You are not
going to cower or be ashamed of what
has not been your fault or doing! That
woman has been bitterness herself ever
since she found out that your mother
rejected Mr Bickerstaff two weeks
before he asked her to marry him. You

give her no time or thought.

'And as for Mr Paignton, he's no different than he was before. You face him and be grateful to him for the position and life you have, for without him your pa would have perished and you and your brother would never have existed at all.

'So do not resent him or his love for a beautiful woman, but if you must mention it to him, then remember to thank him. A lesser man would have thrown your family to the lions' den or the villagers.'

Rebecca nodded. 'It will not be at all easy, though, Samuel.'

Samuel laughed. 'Tell me what in life is?'

'I'll miss you,' she said honestly.

'Samuel will be back before you think about him bein' gone.'

'Tell me about your mama and what happened.' Rebecca saw his face change from geniality to a serious expression at her questions.

'That I will never do. You do not need

to hear it and I do not need to tell it. Live in the present, Rebecca, not the past. It's better that way. Now, I've the master's packing to do and you have to make yourself known or they'll think you have run away after that brother of yours.' Samuel stood up.

'He will return, Samuel. Georgie, I mean.' Rebecca saw Samuel glance at her solemnly.

'I hope so, but then that's hankerin' for the future again. Let it happen. Be content with today, Rebecca — 'tis enough bother for the likes of you and me as it is.' He held out his hand and she took it and walked out of the chapel with him.

His hand was hard after a life of toil, but his heart for her at least was gentle. She would miss her friend, but the prospect of having Mr Paignton's library to peruse at leisure, lightened her heart somewhat.

'Tell me about Mr Luke. What is he like and does he know about me and my family?' Rebecca asked to change and lighten their conversation.

'He is totally different. He'll stay out of your way, when he is about. Anyways, you know what he looks like, you saw him that first day at your cottage.' Samuel looked at her with what she thought was a twinkle of mischief in his eye, but then it was gone and she thought she must be imagining things.

Rebecca stopped and stared at Samuel who had continued about his business unaware of the significance of his last comment.

Mr Luke was her stranger in black in which case she did know what he looked like. Live for the day, Samuel had said. Well Rebecca wished — no, prayed, that tomorrow would be far better, as this day had been filled with unpalatable truths and bitterness.

8

Rebecca wasted no time and went straight to Mr Paignton's study. The cedar wood was warm, yet hard. In some ways it seemed to suit his character in a strange detached manner. 'Rebecca, you have truly blossomed during your time here. I see Cook has been feeding you up. No longer thin and pale. You look just like . . . ' Mr Paignton paused as if reflecting or remembering.

'My mother, perhaps?' Rebecca suggested with a directness that took Mr Paignton by surprise.

'A fine young woman, I was going to say. It is a description that does adequately describe your late mother, on that I would agree.' He rested against his mahogany desk. 'Do I detect a note of disapproval or am I imagining things?'

Rebecca looked at him, wondering what she should say. How far should she push his patience and her good fortune? How could she pretend that she did not understand what had happened between the two of them? It was none of her business yet it had had implications that had shaped her own life, and still did.

'I have been made aware by a lady in the village that my mother's reputation suffered as a result of her connection with this estate.'

Rebecca paused to look at the expression on his face. It did not change. She had no idea of what his feelings were.

'Rebecca, what happened here all those years ago was no-one's concern, but the people who were involved in it or affected by it. I can assure you that no-one acted out of deliberate immorality, only honest love, a tragedy of passion, for which all the participants suffered and have paid for over the years.

'As for the 'lady' in the village, I suspect that there is more malice and revenge in her heart than there was ever in your mother's or father's. Revenge, Rebecca, is an empty folly; do not think or wish it on anyone for it is often the downfall of the perpetrator of such thoughts.'

'Would it be wrong to seek justice against those who were ready to judge and ostracise my parents, or kidnap my brother and desert myself?' She displayed her true feelings.

'Let the Lord be the judge of people. It is His place, not ours. You concentrate on living, my girl. I understand that you have a love of books. You may use my library so long as you have seen to your other duties. I take it Miss Jacobs has instructed you as to what they are?'

'Yes, sir,' Rebecca answered but stared blankly straight ahead of her.

'Rebecca, I shall tell you something and then I shall not speak of this again. I loved your mother deeply, she was the air I would breathe that gave me life itself. I respected your father and, for a time, I was bitter and resentful of him. She would never leave him for me, even though I had all this and he had nothing, which hurt me more than I could find words to explain.

'However, there is one thing I will tell you in case the thought has occurred to you. Neither your brother nor yourself are my children. What happened between your mother and I was both sweet and brief. Now, if there is anything I have not covered ask me now whilst you have the chance, for the opportunity will never arise again.'

Rebecca did not like to admit the thought had crossed her mind because she had loved her father despite his pride that had cost them so much.

'Why did you let the Bickerstaffs have our cottage when you knew how much she hated my father? Why let Mrs Bickerstaff have the satisfaction of replacing us with Emily's growing family?'

Rebecca saw Mr Paignton look down at his boots.

'Your heart is filled with resentment. The girl is pregnant. They could not wait for the new housing to be completed. I did it for them, not Mrs Bickerstaff. Listen to me, Rebecca, when I tell you to let go of what was your old life. Let Emily use what was your cottage. By the time their new home is ready your brother may have returned.

'More important, though, is the fact that you would have let it run down and worn yourself out in the process. Here you have a life. I cannot say what your future holds, yet, that is not for me to say.

'Timing is everything in this world. Your time is to prove yourself here. I can offer you a position here, time to consider all that you have learned. If you do well then you may stay as my housekeeper for now, but if that happens we will never speak on this basis again.' He looked her in the eye.

87

'I shall not repeat this offer or speak in such a familiar manner to you again.'

Rebecca nodded. 'Thank you, sir. I will do my duties well.' She would, she decided, until Georgie returned.

'Good. I am sure you will please me as you grow and learn. Now I have much to do. It is possible my younger brother, Luke, will visit. He is a man of simple tastes but have the blue room made ready for him should he decide to stay.'

'Yes, sir.'

'If he does, stay out of his way. He will not stay long and will not want you under his feet. He is not a man that should interest you. Every family has its black sheep. He is ours.' He stared directly at her and she was left in little doubt that this had been a most serious warning. Samuel had not said so much in the chapel.

Rebecca nodded and was dismissed. She could not wait for him to leave because, try as she might, she disliked being in the presence of the man who, in her eyes, ruined her mother's life.

★   ★   ★

'Rebecca.' Miss Jacobs had heard her return to her room.

'Yes, Miss Jacobs?' Rebecca entered the immaculate room and saw Miss Jacobs sitting primly on her chair at her little desk. Her belongings were all packed ready for the next day when all would change in the house and she would take over. The thought delighted her.

'I have left you a list to remind you of the duties you will need to fulfil over the coming months. You did accept his kind offer I take it?'

'Yes.' Rebecca could see the genuine relief on Miss Jacobs' face.

'Good.' Miss Jacobs stared at her for a moment. 'Rebecca, stay out of the village. There is no point in mixing with them. Their views are fixed and their knowledge and understanding limited.'

The woman was still stern in her countenance, but her manner had softened slightly.

Rebecca could not help herself smile at Miss Jacobs' frank comments.

'I see you agree with me. Now are there any questions you wish me to answer before we leave tomorrow?'

'Yes, Miss Jacobs.' Rebecca hesitated as she was not sure how to phrase her question.

'Well, out with it, girl. It is now or never.'

'Mr Luke Paignton, you said he might visit. Well, who or what is he?'

Miss Jacobs rubbed her tired eyes and then folded her hands on the desk in front of her. 'It is a fair enough question, but I have to say it is not easy to answer.' She looked thoughtful for a moment. 'Tell me what you already know of him.'

'Nothing really. Except he is not like our Mr Paignton and I am advised to stay well out of the way.' Rebecca remembered his dive into the pool and their brief meetings in the woods. She did not wish to say anything of them. 'I understand he is younger than Mr Paignton, but that is all.'

'Every family has their black sheep. Luke is described as the Paigntons'. He is some fifteen years younger than the master; he must be approaching his twenty-fifth year by now. He courts trouble, where he goes it is never far behind.

'Stay away from that one. Luke Paignton is another outcast of the village, for young Emily had set her sights on him, but Luke looked in another direction. He had more expensive tastes.

'In the end he was not wanted or respected down there and was, for a time, banned from his family home. He is able to return now only when Mr Paignton is not in residence. They never meet or see each other; however Mr Paignton is good and clears the man's debts and meets his creditors. No, girl, stay well away from a man like that.'

She wagged her boney finger at her to stress her point.

Rebecca replied, 'Yes, ma'am.' She knew first hand that the information Miss Jacobs had was not correct. She had seen them in the woods together, both Mr Paignton and Luke talking as friends, or at least as brothers. They had shown no animosity to each other, although Rebecca had to confess he had shown a lot else.

'Now, is there anything else, Rebecca, that you wish to ask?'

'Yes, could you leave me your address? If you do not mind, that is. I should like to write.'

Miss Jacobs' smile was warmer than she had ever seen in her time there. 'Why yes, of course. That would be very pleasant and thoughtful, Rebecca.' She began to write it out on a piece of paper. 'You are indeed your mother's daughter — so thoughtful.'

'Did you know her well?' Rebecca asked.

Miss Jacobs did not respond

instantly, then sighed. 'Yes, my dear. We were the very best of friends and at one time the worst of rivals, but we loved each other as good friends should and forgave each other everything.'

'What were you rivals for and what did you have to forgive, ma'am?' Rebecca asked.

'Not what — who. Your father, child. There was a time I longed to be his wife, but your mother was beautiful inside and out. He had eyes for her only. In the end I had a fortunate escape, as he was not the man I had longed him to be. When one is smitten one forgives flaws of the character and makes excuses for many feelings. I should never have been happy with him, but your mother was and that is the important thing.'

'Then how could she sleep with another?' Rebecca's words came out unchecked but in a subdued voice.

'Oh, Rebecca, you have much to learn about both love and life. Love and despair are two powerful far-reaching emotions. They change people, fool people and, if you're not careful, completely destroy people. Now I have things to pack. You run along and leave me to my own devices. Here is my address. If you ever need help, Rebecca, you must come to me. I was a good friend to your mother and she me. I offer that same friendship to you too.'

Rebecca felt a lump form in her throat as she said, 'Thank you.' Deeply touched by the older woman's words and genuine gesture.

But then she added a thinly-cloaked warning. 'Don't repeat her same mistake.'

She left.

9

Rebecca finished her book on the fauna of the woods in England and decided she would turn to the classics next. The last two weeks had been heaven. Cook brought her meals to her on a tray and she looked the other way when she went off to visit in the village.

Rebecca closed half of the house off, arranging and organising dustsheets and shutters. She instructed the maids as to their chores, saw to the accounts and read and walked to her heart's content. She never ventured towards the village at all.

She curled up in the large armchair by the fire and stared at the ornate plasterwork surround. Her small cottage seemed a world away, another life almost.

'Comfortable?' The voice came as if

from nowhere, suspended in the shadows.

She jumped to her feet and reached out for a poker.

'Show yourself.' She stepped towards the servants' bell pull.

'I shouldn't bother with that, Rebecca.'

Luke Paignton stepped out of the shadows. His dark figure and features gave the illusion of him materialising from the depth of darkness.

'Mr Luke! However did you enter?' Rebecca looked to the library door which was in the opposite wall. It was shut firm and she had not heard it move for sure; it creaked when it did.

'This house has many secrets, Rebecca. You can never rest easy here for whatever happens at the Lodge is always found out.' He sat down in the chair opposite, crossing his legs in a leisurely fashion. He held his head on one side, as he did when he was considering her in the woods. 'You enjoy your life here?'

'Yes, sir.' Rebecca replaced the poker

and stood primly. 'Would you like a repast?'

'No, I'd like you to sit down as you were before I disturbed your peace.'

Rebecca hesitated. 'I think I should leave you to your rest, sir.' Rebecca dipped a curtsey and stepped towards the door.

'Why? Do you not like my company, Rebecca?'

His dark eyes stared directly at her face. Her cheeks flushed and deep within her something answered, yes, I do, which was why her head was telling her to leave. She had been warned about the danger of this man. Perhaps it was in her blood, something of her mother's nature that was enticing her to him. Was it the sense of danger, the forbidden desires that had led her mother into the arms of Mr Paignton?

He still stared at her, waiting for response.

'It would not be proper. My position is . . . '

'Not to be compromised?' He smiled

at her, warmly, not unkindly but with more than a hint of genuine humour.

'Yes, sir.'

'Then stay and discuss the estate issues with me.' He picked up the poker and jabbed the embers.

'If you wish.' Rebecca sat on the edge of the chair she had previously occupied, back erect, hands folded on her lap. 'I have closed up the blue, green, china and Mr Paignton's rooms. The kitchen accounts are . . . '

'Most fascinating, I'm sure. Can you ride, Rebecca?' He turned his head to her. His features, like his character, reflected an inner strength.

'No, sir. We have never owned a horse.'

'Would you like to learn'? Rebecca looked down and saw his black boots were covered in mud. Mr Paignton would never have entered the house like that.

'Why?' Rebecca asked.

'Why do you answer a question with a question? Would you like to learn to ride? There are horses here to exercise and it is an enjoyable pastime.'

'Yes, but I have to receive the permission of Mr Paignton,' Rebecca answered honestly.

'I am Mr Paignton, Luke Paignton. This is my family home, Rebecca. I give you permission and I would like you to have your first lesson tomorrow at ten o'clock. You will attend me in the stables without excuse.' He was firm, but polite.

'I have a very good excuse, sir.'

He raised his eyebrows as if intrigued by her refusal. 'It had better be convincing, Rebecca.'

'I have no riding clothes or suitable garment to wear, sir.'

He stood. 'I shall provide you with suitable attire.'

He led the way through the library door and across the main hall then climbed the mahogany staircase to the first landing. He waited for her at the top as he took the stairs two at a time. She knew he was fit and there was an energy about the man, a mysterious aura that intrigued her in such a way that she felt guilty at the emotions he brought to the fore within her.

'Have you been through all the rooms, Rebecca?' he asked as she approached.

'Yes, sir. I am the housekeeper, but I have not pried.'

'I never presumed you would, Rebecca,' he answered with a slightly sarcastic tone to his voice. 'However, I am going to show you something you will not be aware of.'

He led her into the master's bedroom and approached a looking glass that hung on the painted wall.

'Now watch and learn one of this house's secrets.' He slid his fingers behind the ornate gold plate foliage that surrounded it. She heard a faint click and a catch was released. The whole panel swung slowly forwards. Luke took the lamp that Rebecca had carried from the library and lit the lamps within the room beyond the panel.

The walls of the small area were panelled with cream, gold and mirrored doors. The beams of light seemed to shoot from one looking glass to another. Even the ceiling was covered in a mosaic of painted reflective panels. Once the dancing flames settled, she could see little cupids adorned the panels as handles.

He pulled one open and Rebecca gasped as the whole wall behind the door was filled with hanging clothes, not folded on shelves or in drawers but hanging full-length, each covered in the best silk.

'Go on, look, find the riding habit and take it to your room.' She stepped inside and found richly decorated, beautiful gowns. Then she spotted the riding attire. Carefully, she unhooked it from its place.

'Were these your mother's?' Rebecca asked in awe.

'No, Rebecca, they were your mother's.'

Rebecca froze momentarily then

dropped the garment and ran from the room, locking herself in her own bedchamber. She was trembling and her feelings were in a whirl. In her head she heard Luke's statement again.

It was only moments before Rebecca heard Mr Luke Paignton's footsteps approaching her door. Her confusion disappeared to be replaced by resentment and, she begrudgingly admitted to herself, hatred.

The man was cruel in the extreme to flaunt her mother's indiscretions in her face, even to the point of goading her with the trinkets of her mother's . . . *sin*. For that is what they amounted to. She did not need a lecture from the Bickerstaffs to tell her. What joy or pleasure he could take from her pain was beyond her comprehension.

Yet, it appeared he was to pursue her to what had become her own room, a sanctuary away from the village and all the bitterness therein. He knocked quite softly on her door, but she merely stared at it. There was no lock to this barrier between them.

'Rebecca, are you there? Please open the door.'

She did not answer him. For what could she say? She was, after all, only the daughter of an adulterous woman. Rebecca had been made dependent on his family for her survival. She had no other home, no-one to turn to and nowhere to go other than the inn or the workhouse. Rebecca wondered if this was how her mother had felt, trapped, beholden and desperate.

The door opened slowly. Rebecca stood by the window, wishing it was a ground floor one so she could climb out and run. Just to be free and far away from this man and his taunts. She had been warned that he brought trouble wherever he was but Rebecca swore to herself that he would not be her downfall.

His figure blocked the open doorway.

'Rebecca, I do not understand. I thought you would be pleasantly surprised.'

She looked at his expression. It seemed one of genuine puzzlement, but how could it be? 'Did you seek to flaunt my mother's affair in my face?' Her voice was barely steady, struggling to control her emotions.

'Her *affair* . . . ' he repeated and stepped inside. 'My brother loved her dearly as she did him. Closeted away in his own rooms, he provided her with things your father could not. For a short time I understand they were very happy. I was only a child, but I remember hearing laughter in this house and that was a rare occasion.

'I do not wish to humiliate you in any way, Rebecca. I merely wanted you to have the pleasure of riding and the exhilaration of the freedom that you crave.' He paused, observing her reaction to his words.

'I do not *crave* anything, sir,' Rebecca retorted angrily. Again she was filled with the uneasy feeling that he sensed or saw something in her that she dared not admit existed to herself.

Her mother's riding clothes were draped over his left arm. He strode over to her bed and laid them carefully down across it. 'They may no longer be the height of fashion. However, wear them with pride. I shall expect you to arrive for your first lesson at ten o'clock precisely in the morning. Do this for yourself, Rebecca. Let yourself relax, just a little.'

'Why are you doing this?' Rebecca asked, exasperated by the man's persistence.

He paused in the doorway and shook his head. 'I honestly have no idea. It is not as if I have anything else to do. So humour me and do not pass over your chance to learn something new.' He left, closing the door behind him. It was a moment or two before she heard him walk down the corridor.

Rebecca stood for some time staring at the well-made riding habit. After a few moments, when her senses felt numb and beyond her own understanding, she reached out and felt the high quality of the fabric. The next minute she was standing hugging her mother's coat to her. It smelled stale even though it had been hung in a careful manner so as to preserve it from dust and moths alike.

It had no aura or aroma to pull her back into the memory and arms of a woman she still both loved and missed, yet never really knew.

Rebecca slowly and carefully tried the whole outfit on. It was far from a perfect fit. There was more room at the bust and the skirt was slightly shorter than normally expected, but it suited her well. She looked at her reflection, hoping, longing to see her mother's reflection staring appreciatively back at her, but of course that did not happen. Eventually, she lay down on her bed, fully clothed and fell into a deep sleep.

When she awoke the next morning, she was filled with a sense of determination. It was a growing sensation that she had been feeling more regularly of late.

This morning she would meet with a man she had been warned to avoid and he would teach her how to ride. Today, Rebecca was going to step beyond her post and start to build her own future. She had begun to face the truth. Georgie would not return.

10

'Good morning, sir,' she greeted Luke brightly. His riding attire was far less formal than she had expected. He did not wear the costume of the hunt but the trousers and boots of a soldier. A greatcoat of fine quality covered his black coat, although it looked well used. An unfashionable broad brimmed hat rested on his head.

'You look more comfortable this morning. Are you?' His earnest look took her by surprise. What was so dangerous about this man? She could see nothing, but he did suspend propriety and decorum. He was a free spirit and she had to admit she envied him his right to do as he willed and when he wished to. Oh, she mused, what it would be like to be a man!

'I may have overreacted and I apologise for doubting your reasons for disclosing my mother's things.' Rebecca was surprised when he turned his head toward her.

'I merely wished you to make use of what has been a mausoleum for too long.' He smiled warmly. 'Now should we stop reflecting upon what has already been and concentrate on what is to be?'

'Yes, sir,' Rebecca answered, allowing her mouth to relax into a more genuine smile, for after her night of troubled dreams, memories of everyone who had now gone from her life, she wanted nothing more than to bury the past and live again, but in her own right.

'Honestly, Rebecca, if I am to be informal with you, then call me Luke.'

'Yes, sir.' Rebecca's answer was automatic and she laughed at her own response.

He stared at her. 'That is the first time I have seen you laugh openly for months.'

'You have not known me for months ... Luke.' Rebecca liked the sound of his name as the word rolled off her tongue. It felt and sounded right, yet strange to be so familiar.

'I have been aware of you for a long time. I've seen you walk and run in the woods, with your brother, on your father's land and occasionally walk into the village.' His grin was broad as the surprise showed on her face.

'I have never been aware of you.'

'Never?'

'Occasionally, rarely,' she responded, thinking of the memorable meetings in the woods.

'It's my business to be aware of people, Rebecca.' Luke walked two horses out of their stalls and into the stable yard.

Rebecca followed over the cobble-stones. 'What business is that . . . Luke?'

'My business. Now shall we ride or bore the horses to sleep with our conversation?'

'We should ride,' Rebecca answered firmly. Her first few attempts to mount the animal were abysmal failures. She laughed at her own efforts. Eventually Luke's firm hand on her leg helped manoeuvre her into the correct position. She stopped laughing and caught his eye as she straightened up.

To begin with he took her reins and walked her mount around the yard. She sat astride the horse, unladylike, unrefined but practical, for Rebecca soon found her seat and her balance quickly became attuned to the horse's pattern of movement.

He mounted his own horse and together they moved out into the open countryside of the estate. Luke started to trot and Rebecca's horse followed on cue. She loved it, despite the concentration the change in rhythm required from her. Her legs began to ache as she rose and sat, but she did not care, she felt free.

When he led her into a canter within a field she squealed in delight as the air rushed past her cheeks. It was Luke, however, who had to reach across to get her horse to slow down as it chose to ignore the messages she was trying to send it.

'You are amazing, Rebecca. You take to it naturally. You shall be proficient in no time at all.'

She laughed with joy. 'I truly believe I did not know what joy riding had to offer. Thank you, Luke, for giving me this opportunity and your time. I shall always treasure it.' She spoke from the heart and he flicked an auburn curl from her cheek delicately with his finger.

'It's been a pleasure.' He folded his reins casually over his hands. 'Would you give me the opportunity to ride with you again? Then you can treasure my time again.' His smile told her he was teasing her.

'Certainly, Luke. I should like that very much.' She looked into the depth of his eyes, wishing she could determine what really lay behind them.

'Then I shall visit again next week. Sadly, we must return now for I have business to see to.' He guided her horse as they walked back to the Lodge. 'Rebecca, I hope there is to be no resentment, or misunderstandings between us.' He stopped the horses momentarily.

'Why ever should there be? You have shown me nothing but kindness.'

'Oh, I showed you more than that unintentionally, I assure you.'

Rebecca blushed but could not stifle her smile.

'Whatever I have done in the past, Rebecca, was done for the best of reasons.' He looked into her eyes as if there were something he wished to tell her but had decided not to. She could not imagine what it was.

'I do not know what you are referring to.'

'Then I shall pray you remain in that state.' With that he moved them back into the stable yard and Rebecca left him as he handed the horses to the groom.

'So, who's taken to ridin' now, eh?'

Cook commented as she entered through the kitchens. The woman was supervising Millie as she prepared the dough for the estate's loaves.

'Mr Paignton was kind enough to take me for a ride. I've never been for one before, but it was very exhilarating.'

'Was it lass? He's good at takin' lasses for a ride — so I've heard,' she added and laughed at her own humour.

'He was a complete gentleman and acted with total decorum at all times,' Rebecca replied defensively.

'Really?' Cook's attitude changed. 'Well, I must say, Rebecca Hind, that I'm amazed that you of all people would go out cavortin' with the likes of Mr Luke.' Cook wagged her finger at her and had a stern expression on her face.

'He is a gentleman and this is his home. How can you suggest such things, and I was certainly not 'cavorting'.'

'Rebecca, you are young and inno-cent of the ways of this world, unlike your ma.'

Rebecca opened her mouth to rebuke Cook, but the woman put her hand up to stop her.

'Go, Millicent, see to the dairy.' Millicent dropped a quick curtsey and left eagerly. Cooks' tempers could be heard throughout the servant's quarters.

'Don't get uppity with me, girl. Your ma was a good woman in many ways, but when it came to men, she had one too many.'

Rebecca stared at the large fire over which hung the cauldron that Cook liked to use to make her broth. Her mother was no more than a vague memory to her, but it seemed to Rebecca that everyone was determined to mar it.

'What has my mother got to do with Luke?'

'Absolutely nothing. He was far too young to remember much of her at all,' Cook answered honestly.

'Then why should I not accept an offer of riding lessons from him?'

Rebecca was anxious now to bring this conversation to an end so that she could return to her room and her own duties.

'Why? Well, I'll tell you why, girl, because of your brother of course.' Cook opened her eyes wide and looked at Rebecca in a peculiarly accusing fashion.

'My brother was taken by the press gang. Mr Paignton even found out he is aboard HMS Fortitude. What can he possibly have to do with Mr Luke?' Rebecca asked anxiously.

'He told the press gang to get him. It was Mr Luke who had the coastguards take them to the Flagon Inn where Georgie was drinkin'. He controls the coastguards along this stretch of the coast, does your Mr Luke. He pays 'em. You is messin' with fire, lass, and you'll surely get burned.' Cook folded her arms in front of her ample bosom.

Rebecca shook her head. 'He is not 'my' Mr Luke!' She could not believe Luke could be so cruel. To what ends?

Had he not given her his words not more than an hour since that whatever she heard of his past actions, it was done with good intentions. But whose? His? Was this what he was referring to?

'Why would he do such a thing?' Rebecca asked trying to control her emotions that were so confused.

'Why indeed? Perhaps he wanted the Bickerstaff girlie to have your cottage or perhaps he wanted to compete with his brother and have you!' Cook raised her eyebrows.

'No, you're wrong. History shall not repeat itself. What is in the past has gone and I live in the present now.' Rebecca straightened herself. 'I shall not have this conversation repeated or extended. You must excuse me. I have work to do as indeed I believe you do also. Be good enough to send up my tray within the half hour.'

Rebecca walked boldly across the kitchens to the upper stairs.

'Yes, Miss Hind. Walk away, you can't change what's been but it'll affect what's to come. You mark my words.'

'My tray, Mrs Blakes!' Rebecca called back firmly as she ran up the stairs returning to her room. All enjoyment and exhilaration at her riding experience had gone. Her poor Georgie! If only he knew. Mr Luke, whatever his motives, would suffer for this.

She would take revenge for her brother's betrayal, somehow. If Luke thought she was so naïve as to forgive such a murderous act, he was deeply mistaken.

11

Rebecca dressed quickly for her next riding lesson. Apart from sitting on the horse and going steadily around the yard with one of the grooms assisting her, this was to be her second lesson.

She had hardly talked to anyone all week. There had been messages between her and Cook via the maid, but no-one to have a real conversation with. She missed Samuel. He would have told her the truth, Samuel seemed to know everything. Luke had not stayed.

She had received a short message telling her to be ready at the same time but she half expected to find herself alone. However, she had no sooner arrived in the stable yard when he arrived looking as though he had just ridden in that morning.

'You remembered,' Rebecca said as

he walked the horses out of the stable, waving the groom away.

'When I make an arrangement I always keep it.' He walked the animals past her.

She stared at his back.

'You also told me you only ever do things for good reasons. You asked me to believe that.' Rebecca watched as he kept walking, ignoring her speech totally. Cook was crossing to the dairy, and she had no wish to create a scene in front of an audience that had ears everywhere.

Mr Luke had brought her horse to the mounting block. With stiff back and head held high Rebecca managed to arrive fairly gracefully in the saddle. Luke gave her the reins to hold.

'Not here, not now,' he said softly, then pulled himself up into his own saddle. He gave her a few words of advice on how to handle the horse and led them both through the iron gates. Once out into the open country, he moved into a trot which allowed Rebecca to concentrate all her efforts in remembering to work on the rhythm of movement between herself and the horse. They rode to a small copse that overlooked the village.

'You're doing well,' he observed, but gazed down at the village.

Rebecca looked at him, his face was drawn and he looked in need of sleep. 'I would not take the horse out on my own.'

'Nor should you.' His response was abrupt.

'I wouldn't intend to take a liberty . . . ' Rebecca began her retort quickly but Luke cut in.

'I did not mean that you would. I meant that you need more experience before riding out on your own. You could get hurt.' His features softened slightly.

'Would you care?' Rebecca had the words out before she'd really thought out their suitability. She saw the surprise on Luke's face.

'Of course I would, whatever possessed you to think I wouldn't?'

'I have a question which is far worse than that and it may shock you, but I have to ask.'

'Ask then.' His deep eyes were concentrated totally on her face now.

'Did you order the press gang to take my brother?' Her stare was intense. He looked away and her fears were confirmed.

'Yes.'

She felt the tears rising within her, mixed with anger, panic and disgust. She pulled the horse's reins to turn it away from him.

'I did it for his own good.'

Rebecca heard the words and managed to stop the horse. He came back to her side.

'Rebecca, you don't understand.' His voice was softer but not apologetic. Rebecca could not understand how he could even face her, yet he had done just that. Reluctantly she looked at him, he was a powerful man and she was very aware of his strength, both in character and in muscle.

'How can I?' she asked. She pressed her lips together trying to stop the tremble that was threatening. 'How could you arrange for the kidnapping, which is all it is, of an innocent man? To what end? Your family already owned the land!' Her frustration burst out.

He placed his hand on her arm. She tried to pull away but he held her firmly.

'Listen, I've known Georgie since we were boys. We would climb trees together, play in the stream . . . '

'Then that only makes it worse,' she interrupted.

'Because he was keeping bad company, very bad. Rebecca he was involved with a gang.'

'Gang? What sort of gang? He was working part-time at the mill. We were doing well,' Rebecca said defensively, 'until you had him abducted. Now I may never see him again. If he does not return, you as good as murdered him!

Can you live with that?'

He looked away from her towards the village, but kept hold of her arm.

'If that happens, I shall have to. All I can say to you is your brother could have ended his life at the end of a rope had I not intervened. This way at least he has a chance.'

His gaze returned to her face, his eyes told her he was speaking the truth. He released her arm and with a gentleness that surprised her he cupped her chin with his hand and brought her face to his.

'I swear I did it to save his life and you even worse shame. He had got into trouble so deep that there was no getting back had the militia arrested him, and they would have. It was only a matter of time.'

Rebecca pushed his hand away. Something within her responded to this man's touch. A strange feeling stirred within her. Yet, her mind told her severely, you could never feel anything but revenge for this man who had the last member of your family taken from you.

'You are safe here, no-one can touch you. Try to understand that.'

'I don't understand anything of this. Why should Georgie do anything wrong? He worked so hard, sometimes out all night. All he wanted was to help to keep the cottage going. He missed Father terribly.'

Luke put his hand over hers, but she withdrew it quickly. 'Please do not hate me. Georgie was out nights when he was helping with a run of contraband. But he had gone beyond. He was planning to smash, destroy the mill. He listened to the words of the Luddites, Rebecca. The night after the press took him, four of his 'friends' were caught and thrown into the York assizes. Is that what you would have preferred for Georgie?'

Rebecca saw his cheeks were flushed. He was passionate and emphatic about what he had done. She could tell it had not been an easy declaration for him.

'I can understand that you knew Georgie, and you thought you acted in his best interest, but what of me? Did you consider the impact this would have on me? Could you have not told me the truth?'

She was annoyed when he grinned at her. 'Rebecca, I did not know you well enough. My brother has watched over your family from a distance all your life. Despite what your father was, he supported your mother throughout.'

'I know Mr Paignton loved my mother and had no respect for my father, but I asked if you even considered what would happen to me?'

'Yes, Rebecca, I did. Which is why Samuel befriended you and why I did not rebuke you most severely for disturbing my privacy down by the pool.'

'Rebuke me! After such a display! Your arrogance is only surpassed by your insensitivity.' Rebecca kicked her horse and set off riding down the hill. All her anger, all her feelings for this annoying patronising man were driving her beyond her patience. Her situation seemed hopeless. She was at the mercy and charity of two brothers who were as responsible for creating her situation as they were for her protection.

Rebecca decided she would pack and leave, but to go where? Then she remembered Miss Jacobs' address and her offer. But, what of Georgie? Would he ever return? If he did, would she still know him? If even part of what Luke had said were true, she hardly knew him at all.

'Crack.' A shot rang out from behind her. She pulled hard on the reins. The horse stopped and she looked back just in time to see Luke's body fall to the ground, his horse breaking into a gallop in its panic.

Rebecca kicked her own horse and, without thought for her own safety, clung on as she galloped towards the infuriating man who her head hated and her heart felt very differently for. She prayed he was still alive.

12

Rebecca struggled to dismount as the horse was spooked by the noise of the shot. She was fearful that the madman was still out there and might come to finish off the job he'd started, for Luke lay stunned on the grass, but to Rebecca's great relief he was alive. Finally, she managed to dismount from the worried animal and hold it steady.

'Luke!' She crouched low, leaning over him. He groaned, but did not move at first. Blood trickled from his upper left arm. Rebecca looked anxiously around them, but there was no-one in sight. The country looked peaceful, yet somewhere out there was an assassin!

'Luke!' She pulled the fabric of his greatcoat away from the wound. Fortunately the shot had missed his shoulder and appeared to be a shallow flesh wound. It was still unpleasant, but a lot less life threatening than it otherwise would have been. She lifted his head slightly and he groaned at her. 'Luke . . . we have to get you home. Can you move?' Rebecca was controlling her panic, although the worried feelings inside her were building. He raised his uninjured arm and held her tightly.

'Help me to my feet. Then get on the horse and ride straight to the Lodge.' He raised his head towards her and grimaced.

'Where? Do you want me to get the groom?'

With what seemed to be a huge effort he pulled himself to his feet. She took his weight whilst he swayed a little. Gradually he steadied himself with an arm around her shoulders.

'Anywhere away from me. It's me they're after. Go. Now! I'll take cover in the woods.' He tried to push her away but stumbled and nearly fell to the ground again.

'No!' She grabbed the horse's reins

and manhandled the horse until Luke could rest his body upon it. 'Get up.' She sounded as firm as she could.

'No, go!' He helped her up with his good arm. Rebecca hauled herself on to the animal, but then leaned straight back down holding his arm. She lifted her foot out of the stirrup. 'I'm not going anywhere without you, Luke Paignton. I'll not have your murder haunt me for the rest of my life and I don't believe you would want to have mine on your conscience either. You have enough on yours as it is. Now mount this horse!'

He gritted his teeth and glared at her then with an excruciating effort, which resulted in a loud groan, he swung himself on to the horse. 'Give me the reins.' He wrapped his strong arm around her. 'Hold on tight.'

Luke kicked the horse into a gallop towards the cover of the woods. Once sheltered he let the horse slow down enough to manage a narrow path which took them to a clearing in the undergrowth. There they stopped, he released his hold on the reins and leaned into her as he let out a deep breath.

'Leave me here and go back to the house. They'll come for me wherever I am . . . I am a marked man.'

'Then we'll fight them, whoever they are. I'm staying with you, you need my help.' Rebecca surprised herself as much as Luke with the passion and determination she was showing because he looked so alone.

'Then we will have to move quickly. Return to the house.'

Rebecca took the reins. She felt his weight resting against her and it felt strange yet pleasurable. She wanted to help him. Mr Paignton had warned her against seeking revenge. She hadn't understood what he meant but when she heard the gun shot and had seen Luke fall she was filled with fear, fear that he was dead, that the man who had intrigued her, had begun to mean something to her in a very personal way, but fear she had lost him forever before having the chance to really know him.

They returned to the Lodge where she let him slide down in front of the main door.

'Leave the horse and help me inside, Rebecca.'

'Should I ride to the village for Mr Bickerstaff or the doctor in Skelham?'

Rebecca helped him regain his balance as he dismounted. The fall had been hard and so had the knock on his head. Luke stepped forward on his own, and regained his composure well.

'I'll go to my room. Please bring something to see to this wound and don't mention it to anyone.' Luke forced a smile at her.

He made his way to the main staircase and pulled himself up. Rebecca went to the kitchens. She fetched some water, clean cloth to wrap the arm in, some honey and some brandy.

Cook entered, as she was about to leave.

'Fell off it did yer?' Her voice was full of sarcasm.

'I'm sore. I didn't fall off anything.' She continued on her way.

'Pride comes afore a fall, or afterwards.' Cook laughed at her own quip but Rebecca was not going to tell the busybody the truth of it.

The woman visited the village regularly and no doubt gossiped at length to Emily Bickerstaff about her and Luke.

She approached Luke's bedchamber and tapped on the door gently, balancing the tray carefully on her other arm.

'Enter.' Luke's voice was husky.

Rebecca propped the tray against the door as she carefully unlatched it. As it opened she nervously walked in. Luke was standing by his large four poster bed. His coat, jacket, shirt and hat were thrown across the covers. The sight of his naked torso, so close and firm caused her to stop in mid-stride. She swallowed and continued hoping he had not seen the effect he had on her.

13

'Rebecca place the tray on the table.' He moved towards her as she set the tray down and turned to him to examine his arm. The wound was angry and needed cleaning but she thought his disorientation had been caused purely by the blow on the head rather than the wound to his arm, and his eyes were looking clearer.

She used the cloth and water first, then left the honey on the wound before wrapping the upper arm. The brandy she gave him to drink. He took a mouthful but refused to have any more.

'I need my wits about me. This is no time for dimmed senses.'

She nodded in agreement and fetched a clean shirt, helping him on with it.

'Thank you,' he said, as she bent over

his seated figure.

'You're welcome.' Rebecca was surprised as his expression showed he was also surprised by the fact that she clearly meant it.

'I wouldn't have been surprised if you had left me out there after what I did. Does this mean that you believe me? Or at least accept my motives were honourable?'

She looked at him and sensed a huge loneliness and vulnerability about him. Impulsively she stroked his hair with one hand.

'Why are you a marked man? Who shot at you? And why?'

He leaned into her hand. He reached up turning his head, took her hand and gently kissed it. They stared into each other's eyes and their feelings were open and mutual. For a few precious moments it felt as though they were suspended in a perfect silence. Rebecca blushed. 'You haven't answered my questions.'

He stood up without taking his hand

from hers. She let her hand follow the contours of his face, then his shoulder before pulling it away. His lips found hers and she responded. Automatically her arms encircled his neck, then she hugged him to her and was greeted with a muffled, 'Aargh!'

'I'm sorry, I forgot. I didn't mean to hurt you . . . ' She stepped backwards.

'It's not that bad, just tender. I . . . '

'We need to talk, Luke.' Rebecca stared at the man in front of her and wanted to help him but had no idea how.

'Yes, we must.' He took her by the hand and led her to the chaise longue.

'I shall be honest, but you will not like what I have to say.'

They sat together. She leaned into the chaise longue and he perched on the side talking to her, one booted leg crossed casually over the other.

'I work for the Custom Services, Rebecca.'

'A revenue officer?' she queried, not really understanding the difference.

'No, not quite. I travel to places trailing those who would bring opium, slaves and arms into the country. Sometimes my work is hazardous but for the most part it has been enjoyable, until now.'

'Because you have been wounded?' Rebecca asked even though she had noticed scars on his body when she had tended to him.

'No, I've been hurt before, but this time the trail has led me too close to home . . . my home here.'

'The village?' Rebecca remembered the way he had looked down at the village from the copse.

'Yes.' He shifted uneasily.

'My brother's involvement?' Rebecca asked in a quiet voice.

'Oh, he was just a stupid opportunist who had no idea what he was getting himself involved in. I talked to him but he wouldn't listen to me. He thought because my brother owned this that I had no idea what was happening in the real world. So he decided that he would be rich too.

'They'd have killed him if the authorities hadn't hung him first, for the only person he did not brag to about his dealings was you, Rebecca. Someone in the village has to be the link to the main operator because all my sources have led back here.'

'So this is the 'business' you had with Mr Paignton, when you met him at the pool?' Rebecca was able to look him in the eye without embarrassment this time. One kiss could change many things.

'Indirectly, you see we had everyone believing we were estranged. The village knew there was animosity over father's will and my mother refused to stay under the same roof as my half-brother when he inherited all, and I nothing of worth. However, what they did not know is that he is a good man and has helped me in my work by allowing me to come and go at will and use this place as a base when I need to stay low and disappear for a while, should we say.'

'So why are you a marked man? Who knows you are here? And why should they kill you? Surely you would just be replaced,' Rebecca asked innocently.

'If I smash this operation, someone will lose a sizeable income. Also those named will be shamed and hanged. I'm sorry, Rebecca, I should not have got you involved in any of this. It is just that having you here, seeing you so near after admiring you from afar for so long, I forgot myself and endangered not only my life but yours too.' He held her hand in his.

'Did you know I was there before you dived in the pool?'

He grinned at her in reply.

'Immodest of me I know, but I was certain you would stay hidden and my brother would not know you had broken house rules by wandering in his private woodlands. He swims there too.'

'So even in that you were protecting me?'

'In an indelicate way, Rebecca.'

'So, what is to be done now?' Rebecca squeezed his hand slightly. 'We can not let you be shot down like a rabbit. Can you call in the militia?'

'And arrest who?' he asked wide-eyed. 'I think the best thing I can do is wait for my assassin to try again. So you, my dear Rebecca, shall be sent away until the situation is resolved.' He kissed her cheek gently.

'No, absolutely not! I will stay with you. Alone you are too vulnerable. Whoever seeks you is unaware that you have an ally in me.'

'I insist.' His voice was firm, his face set and his humour had vanished.

'I have no intention of doing so and nowhere to go.' She sat upright next to him. 'Everyone and everything I have ever cared for in my life has gone from me. Please don't let it happen to you too, or I shall have the rest of my life believing I am an ill omen.'

He held her tightly. 'No, you are not, you are a blessing, but I can not promise how this will end.'

'No-one can tell the future, Luke. It is for God not man to do that.'

'Then pray it will be a happy one, for after this I shall be resigning. I have a reason now to stay in England and not run away from it as I have been.'

'What is this powerful reason?' She smiled impishly at him.

'You.' His kisses warmed her soul and she could sense hers did the same to him, only this time she was careful not to destroy a beautiful moment with a careless hand.

14

The moment was pleasant and full of promise, but it had to end. Luke lifted his head above hers, sadly parting from their kiss. She saw the concern on his face and the lines furrow on his brow.

'You look tired. Rest now, Luke, then we'll decide what must be done.' She traced the outline of his lips with her finger and he kissed it before standing up and walking over to the long window, staring out into the grounds.

'I have no time to rest. I have to think this through. Somehow, I am missing something.' He scratched his head and continued to view the estate.

'Was it hard to see all this given to another, exclusively?' She stood up straightening her dress.

'Not really, I'm only his half-brother. I lived large parts of my life in a different place. I had a totally different existence. I love this estate, but it is rightfully my brother's.' He turned to her. 'I wish you would leave.'

'No you don't.' Rebecca's answer surprised him, but he smiled.

'You sound so certain; am I so easily read?'

'Not at all, but I don't believe that you could kiss me like that with so much need in you if you really wanted me to go away.' Rebecca moved closer to him.

Luke held her hand in his. 'Perhaps you're right, but I want you to be safe and I am in no position to protect you, as I have an invisible enemy at present.'

'I'll have a tray brought up to you. I'll be in the library if you want me.' Rebecca crossed the room; she wanted to stay, to hold him but she knew better and forced her feet to take her quietly away.

'Becky, you're a stubborn woman.'

'Thank you, but I prefer the word determined.'

He smiled at her, the tiredness he

was feeling etched on his face.

'Thank you for not leaving me. I could not have blamed you if you had.'

'Rest now.' She left him with her mind troubled at the situation he was in. She loved him, she felt she wanted him but history would not repeat itself. If they had a future then it could only be if he was prepared to marry her, but first she had to make sure they did have one.

Rebecca felt his presence as soon as she went in the library. The door closed behind her.

'Rebecca, you look well.' Mr Paignton's voice seemed older than she had realised previously, or perhaps he was tired. He was sitting in his chair by the open fire.

'Mr Paignton, I was not expecting you. I did not receive word of your arrival or I would have had your room ready. I'll inform Cook immediately.'

Rebecca turned to go but was stopped.

'No need. I did not announce my

arrival for good reason. You have kept my house well, Rebecca.' He gestured that she should sit down on the opposite chair.

'Were you checking on my ability?'

Rebecca sat down but was very ill at ease, perched on the edge of the seat.

'Now tell me all that has been happening here — or has it been extremely dull?' He leaned back and crossed his legs casually, watching her intensely.

'Mr Luke is here, sir. He rests in his room. Should I send word that you have arrived?' Rebecca thought about telling him of the morning's events but decided that it was Luke's prerogative. He may not want to concern Mr Paignton.

'Then let him rest. I shall go up later after our chat, Rebecca.'

Rebecca continued to inform him of the matters pertaining to the running of the estate. He seemed quite uninterested but listened.

Then he raised a hand to stop her

talking and leaned forwards.

'Tell me, Rebecca, is there anything else that you would have to tell me?' He placed a hand on her knee and she felt most uneasy.

'Don't be frightened of me, Rebecca. I am your closest friend. Has Luke behaved himself?'

Rebecca was shocked at his inference. His question was so obvious.

'Like a gentleman, sir,' Rebecca said defensively. She noticed a smirk across his face.

'Really? Well he has changed for the better it would seem. The man is a known womaniser and letch. He uses girls like you, young women. He tells them a tale of woe, the unfortunate half brother left to fend for himself, deprived of his estate, named and shamed for the traitor he is!'

'Traitor! He works for the government.' The words were out before Rebecca thought better of them and she instantly regretted her slip.

'So, he has spun you that yarn too.'

He shook his head slowly, regretfully. 'You in your innocence have fallen prey to it. Have you fallen for his charms too?'

'Mr Paignton!' Rebecca stood but he prevented her from leaving. He held her forearms in a tight grip.

'Look at me, Rebecca. It is important that you tell me the truth. Luke is a deviant amongst men, he uses girls like you. You must help me rid the world of his evil. Have you ever heard of the white slave trade?'

Rebecca knew not what he referred to. She could not believe for one moment that Luke was so horrid. She believed in him.

'Of course you haven't. You're an innocent. He steals a woman away to . . . well, that is not your concern. Suffice it to say their futures are not rosy. Will you help me rid this place of him once and for all? Will you?'

Rebecca was scared as his grip tightened.

'If I must,' she replied, hoping not to

have to lie outright.

'Good girl. Tomorrow you lure him out for a ride, like you did today. I'll see to the rest.'

Rebecca stared at him. He was mad, she could see it in his eyes; he must be.

'That's a good girl.' He leaned his head forward to hers and brought his moist lips upon hers and pressed his mouth over hers with a desperate urgency, but Rebecca did not respond. She couldn't for, just as her body had come alive with Luke's touch, Mr Paignton's made her feel like she was made of stone.

When he had finished he looked at her. 'My dear Rebecca, you are a young woman and I shall respect your ignorance in such bodily contact. But once we have completed this unpleasant task I shall take you under my wing. You have proved you can run my household and I am no longer bothered what society says, so never fear. I shall make you my wife.

'I should have done so with your

mother but I made a bad judgement. I shall not do it again.'

He patted her shoulder. 'Go to your room now. I shall see Luke. Tomorrow, we shall put a great wrong to right.' He looked away from her and Rebecca left the room as fast as she seemly could.

The picture that he had painted for her was abhorrent on both accounts. She loved Luke and she would save him. Never could she marry Mr Paignton and she would never be a substitute in his affections for her mother. How could she have loved him? Could she have really known what he was like? Then a tragic reality dawned.

Her mother had no choice in the matter; he owned their land and then her mama. No wonder her father was bitter, and even less understanding was needed to see why the villagers hated them so.

Rebecca ran to her room and prayed she would know what to do, and when.

15

Rebecca returned to her room. She saw Mr Paignton make his way out of the library and head up to Luke's room. She could not bear it. It had to be Mr Paignton who was in the wrong and Luke who was right.

Why ever had he not had Luke arrested by the militia? Unless, she reasoned, it was because of the shame it would bring on the family name. If that was so, was it acceptable to take the law into his own hands? No matter which way she reasoned it, one thought prevailed — Luke was too much of a gentleman to be involved in something so callous. She loved him and somehow she would save him.

Rebecca tiptoed up the stairs. She edged slowly along the shadows to Luke's bedchamber door. She could hear voices, not arguing but talking.

She pressed her ear to the door, as it was an inch ajar.

'You know how much I want to help you, Luke. This grieves me to see you in such a predicament. Let me pay your passage to the Americas. You could start over. Find yourself a young wife and put all this behind you.'

'But who would break the hold on the area? Robert, someone is the brains up here.' Luke was facing the door. She prayed that he could not see her through the crack.

'Bickerstaff? He has influence. It could be him. It would make sense, Luke, he wouldn't be the first corrupt priest.'

Luke rubbed his head with his hands, then his arm gently beneath his wound.

'I don't think so. The man is a social climber, but trader, smuggler and assassin, I can't see it myself.' Luke paused.

'Rebecca! Surely you do not suspect her just because her foolish brother had a loose mouth?'

Luke looked at his brother thoughtfully. 'No, she is an innocent in all of this. I wish to protect her, to . . . '

'I'll protect Becky. I aim to marry her.'

Luke's face appeared shocked at his brother's words. 'You can't, it would not be fitting.' Luke's voice was so husky it was almost inaudible.

'Yes, it will be. I've informed her and it will be done. She is a very fortunate girl. She nearly faced the workhouse and instead she will be the mistress of my house, as her mother should have been before her.' Mr Paignton sounded happy; Luke looked anything but.

'Does she love you, Robert?'

'My dear Luke, how little you know of women. She does not need to. Her affection will grow with time as the children arrive. A mistress needs love, a wife needs security. Rebecca will learn to please me and she will be suitably rewarded.'

'Did she accept your proposal?' Luke persisted.

'I have told her and she will obey me as any good woman should her husband. She is already grateful to me. There is no more to be said on the issue. Now you must sort yourself out, man. Ride tomorrow and I shall cover your back. We will capture the black-guard and then you must look to the colonies and a new life. Tidy yourself up, man. Cook will have dinner ready in one hour and we will expect you down to congratulate us on our future.'

Mr Paignton patted Luke on his shoulder and Rebecca saw his grimace before hiding in the adjacent room. She waited for Mr Paignton to descend the stairs and ran into Luke's room. He was trying to button up a waistcoat.

'Luke, I . . . '

He turned and stared at her. His face was pale as he picked up a small pistol and tucked it inside his pocket. 'He has told me of his plans for the two of you. Congratulations.'

'Don't, Luke. You know as well as I that I can not and will not marry a man who still loves my dead mother. I think he is mad.' She paused, waiting for his reaction but he appeared to be moving in a trance. Rebecca waited for him to reply. He pulled on his jacket and then his greatcoat.

'Luke, what are you doing? Where are you going? Luke, 'he' is the man you seek. He aims to kill you. Can you not see it?' Rebecca's voice was full of urgency but she tried to keep it low. He placed a hand against her cheek.

'Do you love me, Rebecca?' he asked her with eyes that looked moist.

His eyes were filled with sadness and she realised he knew that Mr Paignton was the missing link.

'Yes, with all my heart, Luke. But what are you going to do?'

'Get us both away from here. He will realise where you are shortly so we'll use the passage.'

Luke released a wall panel beside his bed and took the small oil lamp with him to lead the way down a small panelled staircase. 'This takes us to the library, from there we can leave by the window and cross to the stables. I'll give you my coat as soon as we are there. We must not stop for I fear your appraisal of my brother's state of mind might be accurate.'

'Luke,' she tapped his head and he paused momentarily to look back at her. 'Do you love me?'

He turned back to the steps in front of him and, for a second, she felt foolish thinking he would reply.

'Yes, with all my heart, also.'

She wanted to hug him and never let go, but she controlled her urge and focussed on escaping.

'It was Mr Paignton who mentioned I should not seek revenge, but I had not thought of it until then. Perhaps he hoped I should hate you.'

'Definitely, but I never realised that until this day.' He put a hand to his mouth as they came to the end of the narrow passageway.

Rebecca did not move as he released the hidden panel that led to the library.

No wonder, she thought, that Luke had appeared so mysteriously from the shadows.

They entered the darkened room, crossing quietly to the window. By the time they reached the stables she could feel her heart beating within her breast. He saddled up their horses and helped her up.

'Luke!' She stared at the figure of Mr Paignton standing in the stable doorway holding a pistol.

'My dear child. This is no time for a riding lesson and Luke you should be ashamed of yourself disgracing the reputation of my betrothed.'

'Drop the charade, Robert. You have lived a lie long enough. Did you really think you could get away with it forever?'

Luke turned to face his brother, and Rebecca sat motionless wondering if she dared risk saying or doing anything.

'No, I knew I couldn't. Which is why I kept a discreet contact with my half-wit brother. Quietly, of course, so as not to arouse suspicion. You see, everyone knows officials are corrupt. Government men and priests. Yes, Bickerstaff and his accursed wife shall fall too. I have enough in place to point the finger at you both. You work so well together, do you not?'

'He has tried to turn those in the village to a more 'righteous' path, yes.' Luke said and casually raised his hand to the horse's neck.

'You two fools will provide the perfect case. I shall be the hero of the hour and my wife and I will bathe in the glory of this victory over evil. My heritage preserved and of course, in time, an heir of suitable breeding will inherit it.'

'You're mad, Robert. Your wits have left you. It was you who tried to shoot me. You would murder your own brother to hide your filthy trade.' Rebecca looked down at Luke's hand as it rested on the horse's neck. He held the small pistol. She tried to keep the horse steady.

'Of course! You are of no significance. Half-breed, halfwit.'

'My mother was a French lady, her family owned large estates. Grander than this, Robert. Yet you hold her nationality against her even though her family escaped the troubles.' Luke's finger found the pistol's trigger. Rebecca sat still. She was desperate not to give his intentions away. His life, their future, depended on what was to happen in the next few moments.

'The Revolution was just, only it did not go far enough. Bonaparte will win, and in the new Europe my position and allegiance will be honoured. You will be remembered as a letch and traitor. So save your speeches for you are about to meet your maker.'

Mr Paignton's arm came up, but before he could pull the trigger, Luke had aimed and fired.

16

The stunned look on Mr Paignton's face as he fell to the floor and the crack of the shot made Rebecca gasp. The horse reared, knocking Luke to the ground. Rebecca fought for control and the groom appeared at the doorway. He looked at the two men laid on the ground and ran over to Rebecca.

'Thank you,' she said with relief as he helped to calm the horse. 'Please go to the village and fetch Reverend Bicker-staff and then the doctor, and hurry, please.'

He looked uneasily around for a moment as Rebecca collected the fallen pistols. 'Please hurry!'

He mounted the horse and rode out. Rebecca lifted Luke's head, 'Luke, Luke . . . '

'Is he dead? Did I kill him?' He struggled to his feet.

Rebecca approached the prone body. It was obvious he was dead. All the time she had thought of taking revenge against the man responsible for Georgie's abduction meant nothing to her. No man's death seemed worth another's to her, yet this man had once been good or her mother could not have loved him.

He had warned her what bitterness could do to a person, but she had not realised he spoke from personal experience. 'Yes Luke, you did, but it was self defence. I will testify to that.'

He removed his greatcoat and spread it over the body. 'You will not have to. I shall write my report. It will have been an unfortunate hunting accident. There will be no trial, no shame, but after I have cleared his desk of all the evidence the ring will finally be smashed.'

'What will you do?' Rebecca asked. 'Can you live here now?' She leaned her head on his chest.

'No, never. I would not have wanted

to anyway. My family has lands in France and the colonies. When the world is at peace again I should like to visit them all.'

Rebecca pulled away. 'You are indeed fortunate. I shall tell Cook there has been a tragic accident.' She walked to the stable door but Luke caught her arm.

'Is that all you have to say?'

'What else can I? Your future is both secured and determined. There is nothing more for me to do here than my present duties.' Rebecca did not look up at him, realising what had been so fleetingly between them was lost, gone forever.

'I have one more thing to say if you will hear me?' He made her look at him and she shrugged her shoulders as words failed her.

'Rebecca Hind, will you marry me and travel this wretched world with me until we find a home we can both love and adore?'

Her eyes moist, emotions spent,

words still failed her but the kiss they shared spoke for eternity, and the future she knew was all theirs.

THE END

We do hope that you have enjoyed reading this large print book.

Did you know that all of our titles are available for purchase?

We publish a wide range of high quality large print books including:
Romances, Mysteries, Classics
General Fiction
Non Fiction and Westerns

Special interest titles available in large print are:
The Little Oxford Dictionary
Music Book, Song Book
Hymn Book, Service Book

Also available from us courtesy of Oxford University Press:
Young Readers' Dictionary
(large print edition)
Young Readers' Thesaurus
(large print edition)

For further information or a free brochure, please contact us at:
Ulverscroft Large Print Books Ltd.,
The Green, Bradgate Road, Anstey,
Leicester, LE7 7FU, England.
Tel: (00 44) **0116 236 4325**
Fax: (00 44) **0116 234 0205**

Other titles in the
Linford Romance Library:

MOMENT OF DECISION

Mavis Thomas

Benita is a dedicated doctor, but when questions about her professional competence arise following a street accident, she starts afresh as general assistant at Beacon House, a Children's Clinic. However, this brings new problems when she is faced with her boyfriend's disapproval, the Clinic's domineering but charismatic Superintendent, and the two disruptive children she befriends . . . and then she becomes the victim of a blackmailer! There are many urgent decisions to make before Benita's future becomes clear.

TO TRUST A STRANGER

Anne Hewland

When Sara Dent's landlord relin-
quishes his business interests to his
great-nephew Matt Harding, Sara
fears that she will lose control of her
struggling craft shop. And what
— or who — is causing the strange
noises in the empty rooms above?
As she becomes reluctantly attracted
to Matt, she discovers that her
sleepy market town conceals sinister
secrets. Sara must undergo emo-
tional upheaval and life-threatening
danger before her true enemies are
revealed, and she learns who can be
trusted — and loved.

SHADOWED LOVE

Janet Thomas

Following a break-up with her partner, Helen Matthews returns to Cornwall to set up a bed and breakfast business in her inherited cottage. There, she meets the arrogant Martin Somerville, who offers to buy her land. Helen refuses, but she faces many more setbacks before she can realise her dream . . . And is it possible that she was wrong about Martin? Could they ever look forward to a future together?

HOME NO MORE

Sheila Holroyd

Emma thought she would be a wealthy heiress when her father died. Instead she is shocked to find she faces the prospect of having to sell the home she loves. John Burroughs is willing to help the lonely girl with this painful task, but what about Jed Riley, the wheeler and dealer from Liverpool with an eye for antiques? Which man really cares about Emma and which one has other motives?

LOOKING FOR LOVE

Zelma Falkiner

Fleur's sweetheart, Tom, disappeared after being conscripted into the Army during the Vietnam War. Twenty years later, Fleur finds a package of his unread letters, intercepted and hidden by her widowed mother. From them, she learns that he felt betrayed by her silence. Dismayed, but determined to explain, Fleur engages Lucas, a private investigator, to help in the search that takes them to Vietnam. Will she find Tom there and put right the wrong?

RELUCTANT DESIRE

Kay Gregory

Laura was furious. It was bad enough having to share her home with a stranger for a month — but being forced to live under the same roof as the notorious Adam Veryan . . . His midnight-dark eyes challenged Laura to forget about her fiancé Rodney, and she knew instinctively that Adam would be a dangerous, disruptive presence in her life. She'd be a fool to surrender her heart to such careless custody . . . but could she resist Adam's flirtatious charm?